The WOLF'S CURSE

JESSICA VITALIS

Greenwillow Books
An Imprint of HarperCollins*Publishers*

This book is a work of fiction. References to real people, events, establishments, organizations, or locales are intended only to provide a sense of authenticity, and are used to advance the fictional narrative. All other characters, and all incidents and dialogue, are drawn from the author's imagination and are not to be construed as real.

The Wolf's Curse
Copyright © 2021 by Jessica Vitalis

All rights reserved. No part of this book may be used or reproduced in any manner whatsoever without written permission except in the case of brief quotations embodied in critical articles and reviews. Printed in the United States of America. For information address HarperCollins Children's Books, a division of HarperCollins Publishers, 195 Broadway, New York, NY 10007.

www.harpercollinschildrens.com

The text of this book is set in 13-point Granjon.

Book design by Paul Zakris

Library of Congress Cataloging-in-Publication Data

Names: Vitalis, Jessica, author.
Title: The Wolf's curse / by Jessica Vitalis.
Description: First edition. | New York, NY : Greenwillow Books, an imprint of HarperCollins Publishers, [2021] | Audience: Ages 8-12. | Audience: Grades 4-6. | Summary: Accused of witchcraft and shunned by his fearful village, twelve-year-old carpenter's apprentice Gauge allies with another orphan to prove his innocence and capture the magical wolf hounding his every move.
Identifiers: LCCN 2021028134 | ISBN 9780063067417 (hardcover) | ISBN 9780063067431 (ebook)
Subjects: CYAC: Death—Fiction. | Grief—Fiction. | Rites and ceremonies—Fiction. | Orphans—Fiction. | Wolves—Fiction. | Grandfathers—Fiction. | LCGFT: Novels.
Classification: LCC PZ7.1.V595 Wo 2021 | DDC [Fic]—dc23
LC record available at https://lccn.loc.gov/2021028134
21 22 23 24 25 PC/LSCH 10 9 8 7 6 5 4 3 2 1
First Edition

GREENWILLOW BOOKS

To Adam, Jaiden, and Sienna
I love you to the Woods Beyond

To Be Perfectly Honest . . .

I'd rather you walk away now. Life is hard enough without adding death to the mix. Besides, your precious time is better spent doing something else. Wouldn't you rather be fetching water? Hanging the wash? Picking lice from your hair?

I see that you are not to be put off. In that case, we need to get a few things straight. First, I'm not a beast, a monster, or the devil—I'm only a tired Wolf in search of relief. Second, I exist in the shadowy space between this world and the next. I slip between the two, doing things, seeing things, *knowing* things you will likely deem unbelievable. Finally, you must understand that it's not myself I'm trying to save. Or at least not only myself.

Still determined to come along? Fine. But I warn you, the path ahead isn't easy. It will be filled with darkness and despair, and you will almost certainly regret your decision, just as I regret mine.

Chapter One

I trot through the narrow cobblestone streets of Bouge-by-the-Sea, feeling every one of my seven hundred winters. Over the centuries, my pads have callused, cracked and bled, then callused again. My sharp teeth have dulled. The tips of my white fur have taken on a yellow tinge. Lately, I've noticed bare patches spreading across my haunches, leaving what's left matted and dull. Before I became a Wolf, back when I was still a maiden with an entire life ahead of me, I would have been horrified to know that one day I'd be an old, dingy canine. (Who am I kidding? I would have been horrified to know that one day I'd be any kind of canine at all.)

Never mind. It hardly matters now, not if

everything goes according to plan.

The old man's smell is mild at first, but it quickly grows stronger.

When I first started this job, the sweet, slightly harsh smell of impending death—something like black licorice mixed with tobacco—was strangely satisfying. Now it fills my snout, taints my breath with its stench. Not that I mind. Not today. I've waited countless winters for this moment. With the old man out of the way, the boy will be in need of . . . assistance.

My tail swishes back and forth as the Carpenter's shop comes into view. I accept the open door's invitation and slip inside. There's no fire, but the walls block the chilly wind blowing off the sea, making the room pleasant enough. The smell coming from the old man mixes with fresh-cut wood—mostly pine and oak, but I detect maple and cedar, too. A worn counter gives way to a door leading to a workshop that once teemed with half-finished chests, tables, and other furnishings. Now the swept room sits mostly empty while the Carpenter's tools—augers, chisels, planes, saws, and a great deal more—are carefully organized along the walls.

Bastien the Carpenter, once tall and muscled, hunches over a simple nightstand, patiently fitting a tapered leg. His white skin is dotted with age. He's wearing gray pantaloons and a wool tunic, both worn but neatly mended. Nearby, the light-skinned, curly-haired boy of twelve winters finishes tightening the rope he's strung through holes in a wooden bedframe to support a mattress. (This is the first order he's filled all on his own, and he's eager to prove himself worthy of the task.)

My nails click on the floor, alerting the boy to my presence before my scent—which is harsh and wild, more like a stray dog than I care to admit—reaches him. He raises his head and inhales sharply, not daring to say a word. His eyebrows furrow as his lips thin. I've worked hard to acclimate him to my presence. Rather than fear, I catch a whiff of anger. Resentment. (The smells are quite distinctive. Fear is foul, like rotten squid, whereas anger is more like charcoal. Resentment is the worst—it carries the pungent odor of cat urine.)

I can hardly blame the boy.

He first got into trouble during Lord Mayor and

Mistress Vulpine's visit five winters earlier. If the boy hadn't spotted me outside the shop and shouted about the big white dog that no one else could see, if Mistress Vulpine hadn't set sail for the Sea-in-the-Sky that very night, then Lord Mayor Vulpine's Guard wouldn't have barged into the shop the next day accusing the boy of coming up from the Bog and calling him a Voyant.[1] The old man wouldn't have had to beg and plead, and when that failed, trade every shell he had to prevent the boy from being set out to sea. Word of the boy's witchery wouldn't have spread, and he wouldn't be forced to hide on the rare occasions when their few remaining customers arrived.

Poor boy. He doesn't know that seeing me is a gift, that I'm here to help him. Well, maybe not tonight. Tonight, I'm here for the old man. The boy will need time, at least a few days, to accept his loss. To understand his new place in the world.

Soon, his chance will come. I'll offer him a future. A purpose.

I settle into my usual corner, panting harder than

---

1. *In case you aren't familiar with the Gatineauean language (most people aren't): The t is silent, so it's pronounced VOY-on.*

normal as I struggle to maintain my composure.

Determined to ignore me, the boy finishes tightening the rope and trims the excess. When he's finished, he calls his grandpapá over to inspect his work.

The old man runs his hand along the bed's sturdy posts. "Why didn't you use oak?"

The boy knows he's being tested. "Mistress Abrielle could only pay seventy-five shells. Besides, she lives all the way across the village and pine isn't as heavy."

He watches the old man anxiously. His grandpapá used to be jolly, forever telling jokes and handing out praise. After the incident with Mistress Vulpine, his laughter disappeared and his words dried up like water in an old well. The boy can't kindle the spark missing in the old man's eyes, but he can pay attention, work hard, and one day follow in his grandpapá's footsteps.

The corners of the old man's lips turn up slightly. He tests the strung rope, which gives only a little under the pressure of his palm. "How did you tighten it on your own?"

"I used the bed wrench to pull the rope taut, but instead of calling for you to hold it, I stuffed an awl in the hole so the rope couldn't slip while I worked on the other side."

He's proud of his resourcefulness, but even so, he hardly dares to breathe as he waits for his grandpapá's response.

"How did you tie it off?"

The boy answers without hesitation. "A slip knot."

"Just as I thought," the old man says.

"What?" The boy's gaze races over the bed, searching for flaws.

"Carpentry is in your blood."

The boy swells like a tick fresh off a feeding.

The old man rubs the boy's tousled hair. The boy grins but, being tightly attached to the curls he's been told he inherited from his late mother, pulls his head away.

(The boy's name? Oh, for death's sake. It's Gauge,[2] if you must know, though I see little point in calling him that—not when he'll be giving the name up soon anyway. You insist? Fine, I'll humor you this time. But I warn you, don't try my patience.)

A bell jingles at the front counter. The

2. *No, not GAHJ, or anything else you've come up with. It's GAYJ, like "cage."*

boy—*Gauge*—and his grandpapá share a wide-eyed glance. They haven't had a customer all week, and they're down to their last few potatoes—even a couple of shells will provide a welcome reprieve from the hunger clawing at their bellies. (Just so you know: these aren't the kind of shells you can find on any old beach. They wash up on shore in only one location in all of Gatineau, and the supply is carefully regulated by Grand Lord Lasage, who runs the entire country.)

The old man, knowing he need not remind the boy to stay out of sight, enters the shop.

I rise, shake out my coat, and follow.

The Carpenter greets his customers, entirely unaware that I'm sitting beside him. "What brings you two in on this fine spring day?"

Gauge picks up a length of excess rope to put away, but then gives in to his curiosity and edges closer to the door, rope in hand.

"We have a broken churn." The woman's voice cuts the air. (It's not that she's unfriendly, only that she's been hardened by long winters that drag on with too much labor and too little comfort.) "Put it here, Remy."

"Yes, Mama," a boy's voice answers.

Gauge's pulse races. He imagines himself several winters from now, standing at his grandpapá's side. News of Gauge's skill will have spread far and wide, and the accusations leveled against him will have washed away like footprints in the sand. He'll exchange warm greetings with the woman, ask about her day, and give a few bits of candied ginger to the child beside her. Then he'll inspect the churn and offer a quote for the repairs while his grandpapá looks proudly on.

(If you're wondering how I know what he's thinking, you weren't paying close enough attention at the beginning. I already told you: I'm not bound by the same rules you are.)

Gauge reaches the doorway. He won't go in. He wants a peek. A glance at the life he once led—the life he hopes to lead again one day. It could happen. Or at least he believes it could. Hope bounces and bobbles inside the boy, a buoy that gets him through each day.

He holds his breath and peers around the doorframe. The old man is in his usual spot at the far end of the counter, carefully positioned to draw attention away from the door leading to the workshop. I stick out my long, pink tongue and lick my chops. (I can't help it—the old man's smell is growing stronger, more irresistible.)

A chill runs through the boy. Determined to chase away his sense of foreboding, he blames his shiver on the wind coming through the still-open front door and turns his attention to the woman on the other side of the counter. She's small and lizard-like, with bulging eyes and light, scaly skin. A dark bruise mars her cheek. She clings to the hand of a dirt-streaked child, no more than seven or eight winters.

A butter churn sits askew on the counter, one of its legs broken. "I don't have any shells," the woman says, dropping her eyes, "but I heard you might help. Make this right and I'll deliver half a batch of butter next week."

"I can make short work of this," the Carpenter says cheerfully. "Would you like to wait?"

"Wait here? Oh, no. No, I don't think so," the woman says, grabbing her son's hand and backing toward the door. "I'll come back."

Gauge accidentally brushes the rope against the

doorframe. The noise is soft, almost imperceptible. But it's enough. The woman looks up.

Her eyes widen.

Gauge jerks out of sight and presses up against the wall, his heart pounding.

"Never mind," the woman says, frantically reaching for her son's hand. "I just remembered my neighbor offered to help. I'll have her look at it."

"Please," the Carpenter says. "It'll take no time at all."

"No," she says. "It was a mistake to have come. I really must go."

Rumors that the Carpenter's grandson is a Voyant flitted through Bouge-by-the-Sea for years, and that's what the villagers allowed them to remain. Rumors. But it's hard to look the other way when the rumor is staring right at you. The fact that the boy dared show himself must mean that as he's growing older, he's also growing bolder—undoubtedly more dangerous. The woman snatches the churn and drags her son out the door. It slams behind her.

Silence fills the air, squeezing Gauge from the inside out. He busies himself hanging the rope on a nail poking from the wall.

The old man trudges back into the workshop.

I follow and once again settle in the corner. Although I'm careful not to make eye contact with the boy, my fur practically singes under the heat of his gaze.

"Don't pay her any mind," the old man says. "We can't fill up on butter anyway."

Gauge appreciates the old man's kindness, but the fear he saw in the woman's eyes can't be so easily dismissed. It's the same fear that was in the Guard's eyes when he came for Gauge all those winters ago. The same fear that shows up on the old man's face whenever any mention of me is made.

Frustration crawls over the boy like a headful of lice. He wants to tell his grandpapá that everyone is wrong about me, that Mistress Vulpine setting sail right after I appeared was a coincidence. That although the villagers believe I'm a murderous abomination, I come around nearly every day, and he's never seen me so much as lift a paw to harm anyone. Most of all, he wants to explain that he's not a Voyant, that he couldn't force me to carry out his evil intentions even if he had any (which he doesn't). He's tested his supposed power several times by trying to get me to leave. Naturally, I never do.

But the old man made Gauge promise never to mention me again, to ignore my very existence. The last time the boy brought me up was the one and only time his grandpapá ever lost his temper, threatening to put the boy out on the streets if he continued spouting such nonsense.

If this strikes you as harsh, keep in mind that the Carpenter was doing what he thought best, what he thought he had to do—humans are terrified of that which they don't understand. Although the old man can't bring himself to believe his sweet, gentle grandson would ever intentionally call me, he lives in constant fear that Gauge might do it accidentally. He's worried about his own safety but even more worried about losing the child. He was able to save Gauge once. Another incident like Mistress Vulpine and all the shells in the world won't save the boy from being set out to sea.

Gauge's nostrils flare. He doesn't know why I hang around, why he can see me at all.

(I have no idea why he can see me either. Just as I

have no idea why I could see the Wolf that came for me when I was a simple scribe tasked with recording our oral history. Evolution? Perhaps. Coincidence? More likely. Divine intervention by Mother Wolf herself? Doubtful—she's never shown any interest in me one way or another.)

In any case, Gauge wishes I would leave him alone. The wish is threadbare, worn from several winters of use, but he returns to it time and time again.

The old man sinks down on a stool and swipes at the perspiration beaded on his forehead. "Let's call it a day."

Gauge's gaze flickers to the window. It's too bright for closing time. He frowns, noting his grandpapá's thin frame and the old man's shaking hands. He thinks that his grandpapá must need to rest, that perhaps he's catching cold. The boy reaches back in his mind, but he can't remember the last time his grandpapá was ill. "You stay there," the boy says. "I'll finish up."

He straightens the workshop, locks the front door, and flips the OPEN sign so that it hangs upside down. (The villagers believe that if a sign isn't properly flipped in the evening, it's an invitation for me to visit. As if I care one way or the other about their signs. But these people are a superstitious lot and there is no convincing them otherwise.) Gauge offers the old man a hand standing up and is relieved when it's waved off. He tells himself that he overreacted, that his grandpapá is fine after all.

I follow them into the living room behind the workshop, slipping through the door before they pull it shut. (No, I don't *need* to use doors, but I prefer it. I don't know why. Please, stop pestering me with your incessant questions.)

The room is sparse but clean. Two benches border a sturdy table, and a large pot dangles above the hearth. A single straw-stuffed mattress rests on a bed sized for the two of them to share.

Pacing back and forth, I wish time moved more quickly. Hundreds of winters searching for a replacement should have taught me some patience, but now that I'm this close, each moment stretches out into eternity, leaving plenty of room for doubt to wiggle its way in.

What if the boy rejects me?

It could happen, has happened before. In all my winters, there have been only two other Voyants. The first was a child who didn't survive her third winter. As for the second, well, the only thing you need to know is that she refused my proposal and then had the nerve to set sail before I had time to persuade her otherwise.

There's no telling if or when I'll ever get another chance like this. (Not that it's all about me. As I already mentioned, this is a tremendous opportunity for the boy. It's true that I'm not in the best of shape now, but I enjoyed hundreds of winters of good health. Think of all the suffering the boy will avoid if he escapes the painful business of growing up.) I settle next to the fireplace and soothe a sore paw with my tongue.

I haven't eaten since becoming a Wolf (food being entirely unnecessary in my current position), but I still remember the satisfaction of a good meal, the warm glow that comes from a full stomach. I'd like to tell you that Gauge will be experiencing that same feeling soon, but I pride myself on always telling the truth.

The truth is, Gauge spoons the same thin soup they had for dinner last night, and again for breakfast, into two hand-carved bowls. As he passes the old man his food and settles into his spot at the table, the boy takes care to conceal his frown. He isn't overly fond of the soup but his stomach grumbles uncomfortably. He gulps down the broth, hoping that if he doesn't breathe in, he won't smell the onion and the taste will be bearable.

It works, or close enough, and soon his bowl is nearly empty, his stomach only slightly less so. Two bits of potato remain, a reward he saved for swallowing the broth without a fuss. The boy spears the first potato carefully, relishing how his fork cuts through the soft chunk, his mouth watering as he imagines the warm, earthy taste filling first his mouth and then his stomach.

He means to eat slowly but hunger takes over and all too soon, the potatoes are gone. He's used to tightening his belt, but this winter has dragged on longer than usual. Or perhaps it's his appetite that has gotten bigger. Either way, he can hardly wait until the asparagus pokes up through the ground and birds fill their nests with eggs. Best of all, with the snow melted, jobs will trickle in. Not enough to keep them busy as they once were, but enough to give his grandpapá a few shells to trade at market. Enough to add fish to their pots, flesh to their bones.

The mere thought of summer sets the boy trembling with excitement. His favorite times are the late evenings, when they feast on freshly smoked eel and soft cheeses and sometimes even crisps made of fresh rhubarb, when he and his grandpapá dangle their legs off the edge of the cliff, letting their swollen bellies settle as gulls sing and the sun sinks below the far-off edge of the world.

The boy slides his napkin from the table, revealing the initials he carved into the maple several winters earlier. When the old man discovered the markings, he sighed heavily. "There's no fighting the call of wood," he said, ruffling Gauge's curls. "But do try to respect our possessions."

That was back when neighbors dropped by to share meals, when customers stayed for cups of tea. Now Gauge dabs at his lips. "Please, Grandpapá, may I be excused?"

The old man doesn't answer. Sweat shines on his forehead and above his upper lip. His skin, normally the color of warm ash, is now a pale beech.

The boy's worry returns. "Grandpapá?"

The old man lifts a hand to his chest and swallows, his Adam's apple bulging larger than normal. "I'm not feeling well," he says. "I'm going to lie down."

"Are you ill?"

This isn't the first time the old man has felt this pain in his chest over the last few days. The moments passed quickly. He figured them nothing more than indigestion, the unhappy grumblings of an old, worn-out body.

This feeling is different, the tightness squeezing inside his ribs. He can't explain how, but he knows that his heart is giving up, that this is the end. He's not afraid of setting sail, but he is terrified of what his passing will mean for Gauge. He berates himself, wishing he'd done more to protect the boy. To prepare him for a world that doesn't want him, will never accept him.

The old man always knew this day would come, but he never expected it to be so soon. He thought, as most people do when facing death, that there was time. He was wrong.

There's no help for it, not now. He waves the boy to silence as he rises from the chair, breathing heavily.

Gauge tries to hide his worry as he jumps up and places a hand on his grandpapá's elbow. It takes tremendous effort to remain straight and tall as his grandpapá leans on him, but he doesn't complain, not even when they arrive at the bed and his grandpapá clutches his hand, squeezing it rather harder than necessary as he sinks down onto the mattress.

The boy hovers over the old man, helping him settle. Only when his grandpapá closes his eyes does the boy wipe each bowl clean, tend the fire, and then return to tuck a scratchy wool blanket tightly around his grandpapá's calloused feet to prevent drafts from sneaking in.

His grandpapá's sea green eyes flutter open. He beckons the boy to come closer. Gauge does, and the man clasps his hand. "Run," he rasps. "Run, and don't come back."

The old man's hand falls back to the bed and his eyes drop shut.

The boy doesn't move. His insides quiver, making him jittery, restless, and ever so slightly nauseous.

He wonders if his grandpapá really means for him to leave. The old man claims that he's happy—that they only need each other—but the boy suspects that his grandpapá longs for his old life back, for the days when he wasn't shunned, when people flocked to the shop.

The Carpenter moves his lips, willing his final words into existence.

Gauge tips his head. "What did you say, Grandpapá? I didn't hear you."

He bends over the old man's bearded face, his ear to the man's dry lips.

His grandpapá's words are garbled and hardly more than a whisper. "Stay away from the Wolf."

A low growl escapes my throat. The last thing I need is the old man meddling in my affairs.

Chapter Two

Gauge's stomach seizes like a broken treadle. He eyes me warily.

I sit up and pull back my lips in what I hope is a friendly smile, flicking my tail back and forth as I did the first time the boy ever saw me. It was the morning before Mistress Vulpine set sail. The boy had been playing in front of the shop; he'd given his ball a good kick, and it had sailed over the roof, disappearing into the back. He ran around the side of the shop and stopped short when he found the ball in my mouth. "Hey, pup," he said, believing I was one of the village's many homeless dogs. "Can I have my ball back?"

I dropped it at his feet and allowed him to scratch behind my ears. The boy didn't know it, but I'd been watching him nearly his whole life, waiting for the right time to approach him, to begin earning his trust. If only he hadn't gone and ruined everything by announcing my presence to the Vulpines that very afternoon.

The ball incident was back when he still played Chase the Goose and Sardines with the other children on the street, when friendly shopkeepers slipped him bits of rock candy or handfuls of spiced almonds while he was out running errands. When his grandpapá took him down to the sea and the gritty sand stuck between his toes.

After everything changed, the old man did his best to ease Gauge's solitude. He filled their days with lessons in the shop and the endless evening hours with cooking, gardening, and whittling, but the boy occasionally wonders about the friendships he might have had, the life he might have lived, had I never shown up.

Now, Gauge senses something is wrong. Terribly wrong. It's early yet for sleep, but the boy feels unanchored, as if he's floating alone in a wide-open sea. He sinks onto the mattress and curls up next to the old man.

He doesn't know why his grandpapá told him to leave, why the old man warned him about me, or how the old man knew I was here in the first place. The old man's uneven breaths fill the air. The boy debates going for help. But surely, if his grandpapá needed it, he would have said so. He decides that if things aren't better by morning, he'll fetch Nicoline the Healer.

He reaches into his pocket and pulls out his folding knife. It was a gift from the old man, given during Gauge's fourth winter. Because it's the same knife the Carpenter used as a child, the wooden handle is worn, but the sheepsfoot blade is sharp and ever ready for whatever carving the boy's imagination can dream up.

He's tempted to pull a small figurine from under the bed, a fisherman he's making for his toy boat. The boat no longer holds his attention, but he's not ready to give it up completely. His fingers ache to work, but he can't make himself move.

Instead, he flicks the blade of his knife open and shut, open and shut. (The repetitive clicking and scraping makes me want to fling myself off the nearest cliff. But it's not as bad as fingers drumming on the table. Or nail chewing. Besides, it seems to bring the boy some comfort, and he's going to need all he can get.) He rolls onto his back and gazes out the window at the narrow slit of the Sea-in-the-Sky, visible through the gap between their home and the building next door. The first lanterns turn on, faint glints of light in the dusky sky.

When the boy was much younger, he and the old man used to wonder which lantern belonged to Gauge's mother. They imagined her fishing, guessed at what kind of fish she caught, how she would prepare it. Gauge tries to remember if the old man ever told him what kind of fish his mother preferred. He realizes he doesn't know his grandpapá's favorite fish, either. The questions—the not-knowing—bother him more than they have any right to. He promises himself that he'll get answers as soon as the old man recovers.

The boy's eyelids grow heavy. He flicks his knife shut, slides it under his pillow, and falls into a restless sleep.

I reposition myself to gaze out the window, remembering back to when I believed in the Sea-in-the-Sky, when I thought the lights really were lanterns lit by my loved ones. That was before I delivered my first soul, before I found out that my daughter was waiting for me in the Woods Beyond. My heart swells as I remember Émilie's sticky fingers cupping my cheek, the smell of her milky breath, her tangled curls spread over her buckwheat pillow. After all this time, I'm finally going to see her again.

Of course, there were also the sleepless nights, the stinky diapers, the throw-up and tantrums and everything else that comes with small children. But somehow, even these challenges have taken on a shiny appeal, no doubt polished by the soft fabric of the passing winters. A single one of these moments with her would be worth all the shells in Gatineau.

I spring up and return to my pacing, tracing a well-worn path across the floor. Finally, I raise my snout and sniff. The stench of licorice-tobacco fills my nose, telling me the old man's time has finally come.

Gauge's dream is the kind that can't possibly be true but feels as though it is. Still, he isn't scared. Not when the Wolf pads toward his bed. Not when it nips gently at Grandpapá's feet. Not when it tugs, extracting from the old man's soles a small bundle that squirms and glows, radiating a warm, bright light. The bundle looks vaguely like a newborn pup, one the Wolf grasps gently by the scruff of the neck as it pads silently out the door. Gauge tells himself to jump up and run after, but his eyes are heavy, his body rooted to the bed. He's warm, and cozy, and happy to bury these strange images in the deepest crevices of his mind, where they disappear like crabs burrowing in the sand.

Speaking of crabs: I figure the boy is going to need his privacy, and the last thing I want to do is remind him of my involvement in the night's event. So, after finishing my delivery, I pass time digging for spider crabs down at the beach. Not to eat, of course. Though I feel a twinge of guilt each and every time I dig up their homes, there's something about the frenetic movements of their skeletal bodies scurrying through the sand that I find oddly comforting.

I see you aren't interested in the crabs. Fine. I'll fill you in on what's going on back at the workshop. (Don't tell me I have to explain how I know what's happening when I'm not around? Surely by now you've figured out that the universe is vastly more complex, and interconnected, than you ever imagined. The idea that I can only observe what is in front of me is quaint—laughable, really. Now please, can we get on with it?)

By now, the sun is up and Gauge is rolling lazily from his side to his back. He stretches, bumping up against his grandpapá. A faint scent tinges the air, one that's wild and musty. It tickles his brain, and although he remembers nothing of his dream, he senses immediately that something is wrong. He snaps awake. His grandpapá is an early riser. He's never in bed when Gauge awakes. Never.

The boy flips over to his knees and sits up. He rests a hand on his grandpapá's clothed chest. Pale morning light shines in from the window and the boy notes how long and thin his youthful fingers are, how they stand in stark contrast to the dark blue flannel of his grandpapá's tunic, the same one the old man wore at supper.

"Grandpapá?" The boy's voice comes out hesitantly, as though it isn't sure it belongs in the world.

When the old man doesn't answer, Gauge taps the old man's chest and says louder, "Grandpapá, wake up."

His grandpapá doesn't move. Gauge rips his gaze from his fingers and slides it slowly to his grandpapá's face. The old man's eyes are blank, his mouth open. His grandpapá's chest is still. Where it would normally rise as the air travels inside, inflating his lungs, there is nothing. His breath is gone. *He* is gone.

The boy shakes his grandpapá's stiff shoulders as though this might force him to suck in a deep, gulping breath. The boy yells, begging his grandpapá not to leave him. A river of tears streams down Gauge's cheeks and drips onto his grandpapá's face. One of the tears follows the weathered creases of the old man's laugh lines, runs down his cheek, and drops into his open mouth, a salty splash of moisture wetting his dried tongue.

The boy's anger arrives suddenly, bringing with it the ferocity of a summer storm. He pushes himself up and beats at his grandpapá's chest, his fists tightly clenched.

"You can't do this," he yells. "You can't leave me." He wails, his anger slipping away as fast as it arrived, leaving him to drown in a pool of grief. He remembers his question from the night before, knows somewhere deep inside that it's only a small detail, that it doesn't really matter. But somehow, knowing his grandpapá's favorite fish feels like the most important thing in the world, something he should have known—would have known, if he were a better grandson.

He continues to cry, alternating between devastation and despair as the sun creeps high overhead, marking the middle of the day. Eventually, his wet sobs turn into dry, heaving gasps that slow and then dissipate. His sense starts to return, and he remembers that the Steward must perform a Release.

His eyes widen. Without the Release, the old man won't be able to leave his body, won't be able to journey to the Sea-in-the-Sky, won't be able to join Gauge's mother and light a lantern of his own.

The boy crawls from bed and pulls on his boots. He stumbles outside and is blinded by the sun, which he immediately curses. How dare it shine so brightly on such a dark day?

The briny air carries the promise of spring, but a chilly wind blows from the sea. The boy doesn't notice. He's busy tracing a map in his head, trying to remember how to find Mistress Charbonneaux.[3]

She lives in a comfortable home on the edge of the cliff, a prestigious spot befitting the village's only Steward. The boy doesn't know her, not properly. But he doesn't know *anyone* properly. The Carpenter worked for nearly all the villagers at one time or another, but Gauge was kept hidden from them for the last several winters. Ever since the Wolf . . . He remembers last night's strange dream. A whiff of something wild and wet—like a dog—fills his nose. His grandpapá's final words fill his ears. *Stay away from the Wolf.* (At this, my hackles rise. Why couldn't the old man have kept his trap shut?)

Grief and confusion whirl and swirl in the boy like a squall.

He ducks his head and sets off through Bouge's twisting streets.

I'm quite fond of my childhood home and should like nothing more than to give you a proper tour, but that will have to wait. For now, suffice it to say that Bouge-by-the-Sea started as a quaint fishing village selected

---

3. *Pronounced SHAR-buh-no.*

for its strategic location on an outcropping of cliffs. Although the residents continue to think of themselves as villagers, Bouge now extends far beyond the original walls and resembles something much closer to a city, one of the largest in Gatineau (though that isn't saying much, given the country's small size and sparse population).

A beach on the bottom of the west side of the cliffs allows for a thriving commercial trade. On the east side, the sea laps hungrily against the sheer rocks but receives only the raw sewage drained from the majestic homes perched above.

It's to one of these very homes that Gauge is headed. He's guided more by instinct than memory as he stumbles through the streets, terrified that he might be recognized but knowing he has no choice. After crossing the tree-lined village square, he glances at Lord Mayor Vulpine's immense house and then hesitantly approaches the only slightly smaller one beside it. This home isn't the Steward's, exactly, but erected and owned by the village and on loan to her (along with a healthy stipend) for as long as she carries out her duties.

When she's no longer of use, she'll be summarily dismissed and the home passed on to the next Steward. Mistress Charbonneaux is, of course, aware of what awaits her and is making plans for her future comfort—plans that include seizing upon the villagers' discontent with Lord Mayor Vulpine's power-hungry ways, with his demands for ever-greater taxes. Someday, she intends to claim his position for her own.

At the top of the stairs, the boy balls his fist and taps on the door. (The Steward isn't required to keep an OPEN and CLOSED sign; it isn't as if death keeps store hours.)

"Hello," he calls. "Are you home?"

There's no answer.

Panic swells inside the boy and his breathing turns ragged. She has to be home—there's no one else for him to turn to. He knocks again, louder this time.

An aproned maiden Gauge assumes is Mistress Charbonneaux's Keeper opens the door. The smell of cinnamon-spiced apples wafts from the back of the house.

"I'm looking for the Steward," Gauge says.

The Keeper waves her feather duster toward him and raises an eyebrow. "And you are?"

"Please, it's an emergency."

A petite, middle-aged woman in turnip-colored pantaloons appears and rests a hand on the Keeper's shoulder. "Thank you, Abeline. I'll take it from here."

The Keeper—Abeline—curtseys and disappears into the dark of the house.

Mistress Charbonneaux nods at Gauge. "How may I help you?"

A wave of relief makes the words tumble from Gauge's mouth. "My—Bastien the Carpenter, please, I need you to come."

He falls silent, holds his breath. He doesn't dare look the Steward in the eye. She doesn't know his face, but there's always the chance that she might put two and two together, figure out that he's the boy who was supposed to have been set out to sea.

Mistress Charbonneaux pulls her shawl tightly about her shoulders.

"One moment," she says, closing the door on the boy.

He waits uncertainly on the steps, wondering if he

should run. He finally determines that she has, in fact, recognized him, that she has no intention of helping him. He's preparing to leave when the door swings open.

The Steward wears a dress as white as a summer cloud. A white veil is pinned to her head, ready to pull over her teak-colored face before the Release occurs. (This is more superstitious nonsense. The people of Gatineau believe that departed souls are drawn to color and that if they don't cover their mouths, lingering spirits might attempt to jump inside their bodies. In truth, souls are initially blind as well as deaf and not the least bit interested in jumping into anyone's mouth.)

She bends to scratch the ears of a calico cat brushing up against her skirt, then picks up her basket and sweeps outside without so much as an acknowledgment of the boy or his loss. (Normally, she'd push a cart with caged pigeons to publicly announce a death, but she has a strong suspicion the boy is the Voyant whose existence she's heard about only in whispers and has decided to leave the birds at home.)

Trembling, Gauge follows.

For her tiny frame, Mistress Charbonneaux moves at a surprising clip, her shiny black hair swinging behind her. The vessel, a simple boat the people of Gatineau believe will carry the old man from the cliffs of Bouge-by-the-Sea to the Sea-in-the-Sky, arrives at the old man's workshop at the same time they do. (While Gauge was waiting outside her home, Mistress Charbonneaux sent a pigeon out the side window to alert the Vessel-maker.)

Mistress Charbonneaux pulls her veil over her face and offers Gauge a white scarf, taking care to avoid touching him. She shifts from one foot to the other as the crew—four burly boys with skin of different shades but all dressed in white—tie scarves over their mouths and unload the vessel from the cart.

They step out of their mud-coated clogs and follow the Steward inside. Gauge trails them but stops at the entrance to the living room, not knowing precisely where to look. How dark the room seems. How gloomy. A stack of wood rests by the hearth, where Gauge haphazardly placed it the day before. The long table where they took their meals and spent their evenings carving, sharpening blades, and repairing tools sits empty. Jars of herbs they collected from the garden out back wait on the shelves.

Gauge can't bear to bring himself to look at the old man's empty rocking chair. Memories of the life the boy lived before I appeared force their way in, the many hours he and the rest of the children on the street spent perched at his grandpapá's feet, watching the old man's practiced fingers guide his knife over a hunk of wood. As the old man carved animals and figures real and imagined, he told stories of his youth, of the countries he visited, of the strange and magical customs outside of Gatineau's borders.

Listening to those stories, Gauge always imagined he would grow up to do the same—travel the world far and wide and then return to Gatineau to settle down, join Grandpapá in the shop. He never imagined that he'd be trapped, that these four walls would become a prison. That the old man would tell everyone Gauge had been set out to sea and stop taking visitors.

How easily any traces of Gauge's life were erased. One day, he had friends and a future; the next, he was nothing more than a ghost, sentenced to live in the shadows of this very room. Now, his sentence remains, but his grandpapá—his teacher, his one and only protector—is gone.

Gauge forces himself to inspect the vessel. His eyebrows knot together. It appears to be well-made, but they used pine. Surely, something more water-resistant would have been a better choice?

The boy comforts himself with the thought that the vessel will be light—that ought to make his grand-papá's journey easier. Finally, the boy forces himself to take in the old man's body. He tells himself that his grandpapá is only sleeping, but the old man's face has already taken on the waxy sheen of a candle. At the bottom of the bed, thick, yellowed nails peek out from under the blanket.

Pressure builds in the boy's chest, causing an unbearable ache. It's all he can do not to take off running and let his legs carry him far away from this place, far from the horror unfolding in front of him. But no. The boy bites his lip. He has to stay, has to bear witness to his grandpapá's Release. There isn't anyone else.

As if reading his mind, Mistress Charbonneaux

asks, "Is there anyone we need to notify?"

Gauge bows his head, flushed with shame. The Carpenter cut off all contact outside of his business after the unfortunate incident with Mistress Vulpine in the shop.

The Steward is nothing if not professional. She keeps her face studiously blank but reaches inside her pocket and squeezes the rabbit's foot she keeps there. (The history behind this particular superstition might interest you. The people of Gatineau believe that rabbits are clever creatures, tricky and fast enough to avoid even a Wolf's capture. Note the delicious irony in carrying a dead rabbit's foot to protect oneself from death.)

The Steward would normally use her pigeons to notify the neighbors that someone has set sail and then give them time to pay their respects before completing the Release at the Wharves. There's no need for any of that today.

Working faster than usual, the crew loads the body in the vessel and places it back on the cart. The small group winds its way through Bouge's narrow, twisty streets. By now, the sun has warmed the air and merchants have opened their doors, welcoming the wind from the sea. Crowds part deferentially in the streets, allowing the procession to pass.

In a short time, they arrive at the Wharves, which rest at the farthermost tip of the cliffs, an outcropping surrounded by the sea on three sides. Despite the name, the Wharves don't look like you imagine. Indeed, the place is little more than an open field where the vessels are buried after the Release is performed. Small mounds of dirt mark previous burials.

Gauge spent many a summer evening here. As long as he stayed a safe distance from the fence marking the unstable point of the cliff, he was allowed to run free. It was only here at the Wharves that he was safe from the prying eyes of the villagers, who stayed away for fear of the souls that might remain trapped with their bodies. (Gauge shares none of their concern; although the old man was every bit as superstitious as the rest of Bouge, he was careful not to share his trepidation with the boy, and, truth be told, the old man grew more comfortable with the Wharves over time.)

Today, Gauge isn't running free. Somehow—

impossibly—he is on his way to say goodbye. The boy can no sooner imagine life without his grandpapá than he can the end of his own life. His fists clench at the unfairness of it all. His grandpapá was the one person in the whole of the world who loved Gauge. Who kept him safe. Who helped him survive.

Instinctively, Gauge knows that if he thinks too much about it, he'll fall into an abyss every bit as dangerous as the sheer drop beyond the cliff's edge. He focuses on the Steward, on her small, even footsteps, on the swish of her dress against the ground.

The only other time he saw her was when she came into the shop to order a headboard. Peeking from the back, Gauge was impressed with her grand clothes and haughty air. After she left, the Carpenter explained that she was the village Steward, that she'd released Gauge's mother after she set sail.

Although they often searched for lanterns lit by Gauge's mother, the old man was reluctant to talk about his daughter's life, much less about her Release. After the Steward's visit, a longing ignited in Gauge to learn everything he could about the woman who set sail before his first full winter. He begged his grandpapá until one night, while sitting with their legs dangling over the cliffs, the old man told the boy how his mother loved him more than waves love the shore, more than birds love the wind, more than the sun loves the sky. He told Gauge how she'd taken sick, how she'd been claimed by death long before her time. He explained how the Steward released her.

But I don't need to give you all the details, not when you're about to see for yourself. See how the Wharves are guarded by a tall iron fence? Inside, a handful of empty holes are kept ready. The four young men unload the old man's vessel from the cart, rest it carefully on the ground, and scurry off to procure ropes and shovels from a lean-to in the corner.

Mistress Charbonneaux sets down her basket. After glancing over her shoulder, she rummages inside the basket and rises, holding a round mirror. She holds it over the Carpenter's face, capturing his soul in its reflective surface.

If Gauge were paying attention, he might notice her pinched mouth, her hurried movements, her care in holding the mirror so only the seashell-crusted back is visible. If he were paying attention, he might notice the foul smell of fear lingering in the air. Instead, he stares blankly at the old man's stiff body, mesmerized by the sleeve of his grandpapá's shirt fluttering in the wind.

"I hereby release you from Bouge-by-the-Sea," Mistress Charbonneaux chants, her words more clipped than usual. "May you reach the Sea-in-the-Sky and sail into eternity."

"Bon voyage," Gauge murmurs.

Mistress Charbonneaux's face strains with the effort of cracking the mirror. Her lips press together so tightly that they disappear. Finally, the glass breaks in two. She rests the pieces on the old man's chest, then returns to her basket and rummages for the final items needed to seal the release of the Carpenter's soul from his body. "Where in the starfish are my feathers?"

Gauge searches his mind, remembers his grandpapá telling him how feathers helped his mother fly up to the Sea-in-the-Sky. (Yes, I realize this makes little sense in light of the fact that the old man is about to be buried in a vessel built for floating on water, but I think we've established that the people of Gatineau aren't particularly concerned about technicalities.)

As if on cue, a single raven flies overhead and squawks angrily. Mistress Charbonneaux freezes. A single black feather floats to the ground. She spins to Gauge.

"You!" The word is loaded with fury. With *fear*. It's an accusation and a question all in one.

"What?" Gauge asks, confused. (Since his grand-papá was careful never to speak of anything related to me, the poor boy has no idea that the villagers believe ravens are a sign that I'm nearby.)

"You called the Wolf."

Lines appear in the boy's forehead as he attempts to make sense of the Steward's words.

He couldn't possibly have called me. He doesn't even know *how* to call me. He'd be glad never to see me again. "No, I didn't!"

"I knew it," she hisses. "I knew you were trouble. Now look what you've done, putting all our lives on the line."

Poor Gauge scans the Wharves.

Spotting not even the smallest sign of me, he's more confused than ever.

"Let's go." The Steward grips her basket. The four

boys behind her have already dropped the ropes and shovels and are wheeling the cart toward the exit.

"Wait, stop!" Gauge calls. He rips his scarf from his face as he jogs after them. "You have to finish the Release."

They exit the gate without looking back, leaving Gauge alone save for the single raven circling overhead. The old man has no hope of soaring up to the Sea-in-the-Sky. Without help, he'll be left to sink to the Bog, where the souls not light enough to reach the Sea-in-the-Sky end up. The boy knows little of the Bog save that it's dark and frightening, ruled by Voyants obsessed with power, with terrorizing all in their realm.

He falls to his knees, remembering how gently his grandpapá held his head up and spooned warm broth into his mouth when he was sick. How tenderly the old man cleaned Gauge's thumb when his folding knife slipped. How he stood up to Lord Mayor Vulpine's Guard and refused to hand Gauge over.

The boy vows to finish the old man's Release.

Chapter Three

Perhaps I should step in and explain that the Carpenter
is safe in Mother Wolf's den and faring quite well,
despite his grief at having abandoned his grandson at
such a tender age. Perhaps in young Gauge's heartache,
the news would come as a relief. Perhaps he'll take my
spot out of gratitude.

But no. Look at the anger on the boy's face. The
determination. He's going to do right by his grandpapá and there isn't anything I, or anyone else, can
say to change his mind. Better to let him go through
with it, to make some sort of peace with the old man's
death, to realize how well and truly alone he is in the
world. Then he will listen. Then he will realize that
my proposal makes sense—for both of us.

The boy rises to his feet, his one thought to secure the feathers needed for the old man to begin his journey. He picks up the raven feather and runs his finger over the soft vane, wondering where he can get more.

At first, he thinks he'll head for the beach, where there must be at least a few gull feathers for the taking. Then he remembers the feather-girl who came into the Carpenter's shop over the winter. Instead of the pantaloons favored by most of Bouge, she wore a long, flowing skirt. It was fitted all the way around with deep pockets stuffed with feathers of all sizes and colors.

Gauge wasn't allowed to help her, but he listened from the back as the girl requested a cane for her father. She explained that Woolsey the Blacksmith had suddenly developed trouble with his balance. After the Carpenter sent her away with his best cane for only half the price, he told Gauge that trouble with balance is one of the first signs of the wasting disease. When Gauge asked about the feathers, the old man said that the girl spent her days collecting them to sell to the Steward.

Gauge wonders how he might find her. He thinks

back to the days before his confinement, when he was allowed to race up and down the streets chasing balls and playing Lucky Rabbit. (Don't trouble yourself with the rules of this game; it's wholly irrelevant to the matter at hand.)

The boy focuses on one street in particular. It's dark and cramped, set back from the cliffs, near the ancient stone wall erected to protect the village from land-based attacks by other countries—a street not far from his grandpapá's shop.

In his mind, he can see the Blacksmith's sign hanging from a well-kept building. He can even picture the forge, visible through the wide double doors that were open even in the worst of weather.

He exits the Wharves and stumbles through the village. This time, he's overwhelmed by the commotion around him. Colorfully dressed villagers hurry to and from their tasks, vendors wander the streets selling everything from apple tarts and sweet wine to pickled sardines and rabbits' feet, and mangy dogs fight over scraps of food. The boy passes a fat cat regally grooming its amber coat. He squints into the bright sun, wishing it would disappear behind a thick blanket of clouds. His stomach grumbles. The boy welcomes the discomfort, feels that he deserves it.

He travels first to his grandpapá's shop (now Gauge's shop, although he's yet to start thinking of it that way), hoping to find a shell for payment. But the Carpenter was a kindly man, forever taking the few orders they received on credit and neglecting to follow up on payments due. And on the day before his passing, indeed for several days prior, he hadn't taken in payment of any sort.

Gauge grips the countertop. He *must* find feathers for his grandpapá's Release. He rushes outside, desperate to find the feather-girl, desperate to convince her to help him. He arrives at the smithy in short order. The doors are closed, the forge still. A weathered sign hangs overhead. Could the Blacksmith be out of business? Or worse—could he have set sail?

The boy studies the dark storefront. Before ringing the bell, he decides to check if anyone is around the back. Perhaps they are preparing the garden for planting.

The alley behind the Blacksmith's property is the same as every other in Bouge—dark and smelly.

Gauge hurries along, doing his best to avoid the sewage and scraps tossed carelessly on the ground.

He stops behind what can only be the Blacksmith's yard. Hunks of scrap metal are stacked by the back door along with piles of discarded tools. A chamber pot crouches in the corner, and a small garden plot claims the rest of the yard.

The boy lets out a disappointed puff of air. He should have known—it's too early in the season to worry about a garden. A pang fills his chest as he thinks about the garden plot waiting for him back at the workshop. Even after Mistress Vulpine, Gauge and his grandpapá used to slip out after dark and work the soil by the light of the moon. They planted seeds, watered the tender sprouts that poked from the earth, and chased away the weeds until the vegetables and herbs were ready for harvest.

The old man taught Gauge how to pickle vegetables, which herbs to dry and which taste best fresh. Though they worked silently for fear of drawing anyone's attention, the hours he spent with his grandpapá outside, breathing in the fresh air and soaking in the soft light of the lanterns, are among the boy's fondest memories.

He remembers the old man placing a lady beetle on his small hand and watching it crawl up his wrist. How delighted he was when the beetle spread her wings and showed off her gift of flight. He remembers the joy in discovering green tendrils shooting up through the soil, in finding long, fat worms wiggling deep in the earth. *Doing the work for us,* Grandpapá always said.

The boy wonders if he'll ever be up to gardening again. *Not without Grandpapá,* he thinks. It's probably a good thing this garden isn't growing; Gauge isn't sure he would be able to stop himself from stomping every plant into the ground.

He sucks in a deep breath and forces himself to scan the rest of the area. A thin rope running the length of the property—from the back of the building to a spindly tree at the alley—captures his attention. Dozens of feathers are attached to the rope with curious pinching devices, all carved from different types of wood, as if whoever carved them used whatever was available. Fascinated, the boy steps closer.

The design is one he never encountered before. His

mind races with possibilities. The pinchers could be used for any number of things—hanging strips of fish and laundry to dry, holding seams together while sewing, perhaps even eating. The poorly tied knot causes the rope to slip lower on the tree to which it is tied, dragging the pinchers—and the feathers— ever closer to the only partially thawed, muck crusted ground. Gauge glances at the building, wondering if the feather-girl is home. He considers knocking but something holds him back. If she says no, what will he do? The feathers dangle in front of him, tempting him.

The old man raised Gauge with a strict code of honor. Under normal circumstances, he would never consider taking something not rightfully his. But these are not normal circumstances. His grandpapá's soul hangs in the balance. He can't risk the girl not being home or, worse, not sharing the feathers.

Besides, it can't rightfully be considered stealing if he intends to pay her back, can it? Gauge's conscience fusses. He searches the property for ideas, for some way to set his actions right. Again, the rope slips. Two feathers rest on the muddy ground.

The boy unties the rope from the tree. He raises it to shoulder height and pulls it taut, lifting the feathers. Next, he makes a fisherman's knot, ensuring the rope won't slip again. Grandpapá would be pleased with his work. His breath catches. He shakes his head, fighting the pain in his chest. He can't handle thinking about the old man's absence—not now.

The down payment assuages his guilt, allows him to collect a handful of feathers from the line. The feathers are different sizes and colors but each one is soft, its shaft sturdy. He stops when his bundle is about the size the Steward held in her fist before fleeing the Wharves. As he backs out of the yard, he eyes the door, hoping the feather-girl doesn't choose this moment to appear. The last thing he wants is to be branded a thief and set out to sea in a raft with no paddle.

(You might think this a bit harsh for petty theft, but thievery is not tolerated in Bouge, and Lord Mayor Vulpine has set people out to sea for less.)

Gauge hurries for the Wharves, thinking of nothing but completing his mission. His oblivion lasts all the way until he reaches the square, where a thick crowd prevents him from making his way forward without a great deal of effort. At last, the boy is forced to raise his head, to seek out the source of the commotion.

Lord Mayor Vulpine stands on a raised platform on the edge of the square. Ever eager for the chance to flaunt his wealth, he's wearing his very best pantaloons—the ones made entirely of a shimmering maroon silk—and an emerald-colored velvet jacket. The white flesh on his neck protrudes over his too-tight collar. (As he dressed, he imagined his outfit was the sort of pairing his beloved wife might have made. In reality, Mistress Vulpine possessed uncommonly good fashion sense and would undoubtedly burn down the Woods Beyond if she saw what he was wearing.)

Lord Mayor Vulpine's face is bright red and damp with sweat. A vein pulses angrily in his temple. Nonetheless, his chest puffs as he points his cane, bestowing what he believes to be gracious greetings on those he recognizes (or deems important enough to deserve his acknowledgment).

Gauge turns his attention from Lord Mayor

Vulpine and scans the crowd, trying to make sense of the gathering. Ladies clutch shawls hastily thrown on over their aprons. Men stand with their arms folded. Children cling to their parents' legs and babies cry. A giant bonfire blazes in the center of the square, filling the air with the scent of dried pine.

The boy realizes he's stumbled into an assembly. He groans, remembering how his grandpapá came home furious after the last assembly, how he stewed about the new law requiring all households to pay for their own vessels to release those who set sail.

Prior to that, the village paid a fixed fee for all the vessels. Lord Mayor Vulpine justified the Vessel Proclamation by claiming the budget could no longer sustain such a practice.

This may be true, but Gauge's grandpapá pointed out that Ruben the Vessel-maker was Lord Mayor Vulpine's dearest friend and surely benefited from his sudden ability to negotiate prices. (It's quite a racket, especially when you consider that there should be more Vessel-makers in a thriving port the size of Bouge. Not to say that Vessel-makers don't pop up here and there, but they always end up closing after

they inexplicably fail to curry the Steward's favor—
her favor, of course, being tied to her dependence on
Lord Mayor Vulpine.)

Gauge reaches further back in his memory, searching for the last assembly he attended. A boy of about
six winters, he stood in the square until his feet ached
and his eyes blurred, listening as Lord Mayor Vulpine,
ever in love with the sound of his own voice and
inclined to wax poetic about his many great accom-
plishments, droned on.

There was a woman at the front, standing tall and
proud. Gauge didn't know why she was there, but
he joined in the cheering that came at the end of the
assembly, swept up by the energy of the crowd. His
grandpapá settled a hand on Gauge's shoulder and
gently encouraged him to quiet. "One never knows
who will be accused next," he murmured, taking care
to keep his voice low.

Now Gauge's heart thumps wildly in his chest,
protesting the precious time this delay will cost him.
Squeezing the feathers in his fist, he backs through
the crowd, intending to make his way around the
edge of the market and continue along a less direct,

but at the moment more efficient, side street.

The crowd closes in around him, slowing his retreat. His breath comes in faster puffs as the throng of warm bodies and excited voices overwhelms his senses. He needs to escape. He becomes increasingly desperate, drawing angry comments and irritated glances as he elbows and squirms his way toward freedom. He's still trapped when Lord Mayor Vulpine begins speaking. The boy has no intention of remaining in the square, but he can't help hearing as he continues to fight his way out.

"Ladies and gentlemen, good citizens of Bouge-by-the-Sea," Lord Mayor Vulpine begins, his jowls shaking as he speaks. "I apologize for interrupting your day for this emergency assembly. As you all know, Grand Lord Lasage, Overlord of Gatineau, charged me with the safety and smooth functioning of our beloved village." (Grand Lord Lasage resides in the capital. A lazy man, he can't be bothered with happenings on the far side of the country, leaving Lord Mayor Vulpine to run the village as he sees fit.)

Gauge's lips tighten as he thinks about how this speech would aggravate his grandpapá. The old man couldn't stand how Lord Mayor Vulpine touted his power and connections. How he used them to squeeze the villagers for ever-higher taxes.

Lord Mayor Vulpine continues. "One of my primary missions has been enforcing the laws of our village, ensuring the safety of all of our residents. I don't need to remind you of the ever-present dangers we face, not only from enemies off our shores but from those within our very own walls."

Gauge rolls his eyes and continues to make his way through the crowd as Lord Mayor Vulpine pats himself on the back for providing the residents a safe, crime-free village. What a load of fish guts! The village hasn't been in danger of attack from the outside for decades. And thieving—no one would dare.

The boy is suddenly aware of the feathers gripped in his fist. His cheeks burn. The feathers are different— he didn't break in anywhere. And he'll replace them the first chance he gets.

He's busy reassuring himself that he's no thief when Lord Mayor Vulpine pauses. It's only when he's assured of everyone's attention that he resumes, a note of solemnity in his voice. "And now we come to the matter before us today. It's with great trepidation that I must inform you that a Voyant has been discovered in our midst."

The crowd titters and shuffles uncomfortably, wondering who among them might be accused. Over the years, a number of people have been sentenced, each and every one of them set out to sea.

As I already mentioned, there have been only three Voyants during my seven-hundred-winter tenure; two of the three died of natural causes. One is very much alive. It also bears mentioning that the accused are nearly always those who find themselves on Lord Mayor Vulpine's bad side.

Make of this what you will, but please, do not confuse being set out to sea with setting sail. Being set out to sea is a death sentence; Lord Mayor Vulpine quite literally sets the accused out to sea in a boat with no paddles, whereby they either die of the elements or drown trying to swim to land. (On occasion, they are eaten by sharks before drowning. But you get the idea.) Setting sail is the journey upon which the departed soul leaves its body and, according to the villagers, begins traveling to the Sea-in-the-Sky.

A deep sense of dread settles in Gauge's bones. He tries to avoid stepping on toes as he continues edging through the crowd. Lord Mayor Vulpine holds up his hand, calling for silence.

"What's more, I regret to inform you that I have upon good sources confirmed that the Voyant called the Wolf to us this very day."

"It's true," a man's voice calls out. "I spotted Wolf tracks when I was out hunting this morning."

"I knew that was a howl I heard last night," a woman shouts at her partner. (There are enough wild wolves prowling the country to ensure that the villagers' fears are never entirely without some basis, however much of a stretch it may be to believe that these ordinary wolves have anything to do with me.)

A roar fills the air as the villagers take in this news. Panic grips the crowd. Couples cling together and squeeze their children tight. The boy pushes and shoves his way through the masses.

Lord Mayor Vulpine calls for quiet. "It is with this in mind that I must issue an arrest warrant for Gauge the Apprentice, grandson of Bastien the Carpenter, who was released this morning."

(You and I know the Steward didn't finish the Release, but she was careful not to share this little detail with Lord Mayor Vulpine.)

Gauge hears his name being called the way one might fall asleep in a quiet room but wake up in the midst of a party—the sound is distorted, confusing. Overwhelming. He can't think, knows only that he must escape.

Lord Mayor Vulpine continues. "Anyone with information on his whereabouts is hereby directed to report to me at once. We have reason to believe he may attempt to make his way to the Wharves. He was last seen wearing dark pantaloons and a gray tunic. A hefty reward will be offered for his capture. Before we part, I must remind you that this boy, this *Voyant*, is extremely dangerous. Indeed, he has already caused at least one death in our village."

Lord Mayor Vulpine's voice cracks at the reference to his late wife, whose likeness he still carries in his breast pocket. (There's also a good amount of anger in his voice, which is only natural given the recent discovery that one of his Guards betrayed him. Fortunately, the Guard in question fell in love and moved to a small farm shortly after accepting the Carpenter's bribe. Lord Mayor Vulpine will undoubtedly attempt to hunt the man down to punish him, but that's none of our concern.)

Lord Mayor Vulpine clears his throat and continues. "It's imperative that the Voyant be found at once. I bid you all a good day and smooth sailing."

"Bon voyage," the crowd murmurs reflexively.

The mass of warm bodies begins to break up and the boy is nearly free when a strong hand grips his elbow, forcing him to stop.

Gauge recognizes the man, though he can't recall his name. The man came into his grandpapá's shop over the winter, demanding a new washstand. When the old man didn't have one on hand, the man raged at the Carpenter for his incompetence before declaring he'd take his business elsewhere and storming out.

"Men like that," the Carpenter said afterward, "aren't worth the shells they offer." (The man's name is Didier the Fisherman. He's the husband of the bruised woman who came into the shop with her butter churn earlier. That should tell you everything you need to know about his character.)

"You're the boy," the man growls.

"I'm not," Gauge protests, tugging at his arm.

"You spied on me from the back of Bastien the Carpenter's shop." The man's voice commands attention. Those around them stop and turn, drawn by the commotion.

"That's him," someone gasps. "That's the Voyant!"

Gauge, realizing he has precious few moments to make a break for freedom, does the only thing he can think of. He stretches the feathers to the tip of the man's nose and tickles lightly.

The man, caught entirely unaware, releases the boy's hand to swipe at his nose and then sneezes three times in quick succession. He claps his hand over his mouth, his eyes wide. Gauge breaks free and sprints through the crowd, darting in and out and around the bodies blocking his way.

"Catch that boy," the man yells behind him.

Hands reach for Gauge, but he dodges them with clever twists and turns, like a fish fleeing a net.

The boy's feet hit the cobblestone pavers. He focuses on putting as much distance between himself and the man as possible. He peeks back. The man has recovered from his surprise and is giving chase, shoving people aside in his haste. Gauge pumps his arms faster and soon finds himself in front of his grandpapá's shop.

Unfortunately, Lord Mayor Vulpine's Guards have already begun searching for the Voyant. It takes only a fraction of a second for Gauge to see the windows have been shattered, the door flung open.

A wave of anger hits Gauge, nearly knocking him to his knees. Instead, he gathers the anger, uses it to propel himself forward. He approaches a familiar corner and risks another glance over his shoulder. His pursuer now lags some distance behind. Gauge turns onto Woolsey the Blacksmith's street, running, running, running, sucking breath into his lungs.

Halfway down, a door opens. A head pokes out, followed by a brown hand beckoning him inside. It occurs to Gauge that this could be a trap. He peeks back. The large man hasn't yet rounded the corner behind him. The boy dives inside the open door and lands on his stomach.

The feather-girl slams the door and crouches beside Gauge, a single finger to her lips. Her panting suggests she arrived seconds before Gauge. He attempts to calm his labored breathing. Moments later, footsteps pound past, then fade.

Gauge scoots so that his back touches the door. "What do you want?"

"What makes you think I want anything?" The feather-girl's eyebrows stitch together.

Gauge's behavior is terrible. But everything he knows and loves is gone. The entire city is hunting for him. If this girl helped him, it can only be because she doesn't understand who he is—what he is. A Voyant.

The word tastes sour on his tongue.

Anger bubbles inside him, stewing and brewing and ready to boil over with only the slightest provocation. The girl (I may as well tell you her name is Roux,[4] since it appears she's going to be part of our story and I know you care about such things) rises and tugs the woven shades down over the windows flanking the door, guaranteeing their privacy.

Gauge watches warily as she moves to the back of the shop, which is filled with stacks of metal, pliers, hinges, horseshoes, and every other manner of item

---

4. *No, not Rocks. ROO. Really, by now you should have started to catch on.*

awaiting repair. Her shirt, the bright blue color of a damselfish, stands out in the dark room.

"There's a fresh pot of soup in the back," she says briskly. "You can stay or go, as you wish."

The boy wants to go—has to go—but can't bring himself to move, to venture back out on the street where he'll surely be recognized, arrested, and set out to sea.

The living room is set up much like the one behind his grandpapá's shop, although there is one major difference: a man with black-walnut-colored skin hunches in a small armchair by the fire. A cane—the one purchased from the Carpenter—rests beside him. Gauge remembers his grandpapá whittling the stick down to size, remembers the old man debating what designs to carve along the body. Eventually, he settled on a tangle of leaves and flowers with a small rabbit crouched on top. He'd been proud of the final product, and rightly so—the cane is every bit as handsome as Gauge remembers.

He can't wait to tell his grandpapá that the cane is being put to good use.

Gauge's heart seizes as if the tip of the cane poked

right through it. His grandpapá will never hear news of the cane, never make another cane. The boy wonders if it'll always be like this—if every little thing will remind him of his grandpapá for as long as he lives. It's too much.

The boy swallows his grief, locks it deep in his chest.

He can't afford to drown in self-pity. He has to stay sharp, do what he must to survive. He forces himself to study the man, tries to determine if he can be trusted. His grandpapá always says—*said*, he reminds himself, ignoring the stabbing in his chest—that you can learn everything you need to know about a piece of furniture by the way it's put together. Under his guidance, Gauge learned how to make a sturdy chair and a table fit for the Lord Mayor himself. He can repair a chest, make grooves and joints meet without a hair of space between them, and carve a figure so real it might start talking.

But people—they aren't as easy to figure out. The man's large frame appears shrunken in size, leaving saggy skin hanging from his body. He coughs, raspy and wet, as if his lungs are water-soaked sponges.

"Greetings," he says. Again he coughs, as though the words cost him precious air.

"I'm Roux, and this is my father, Woolsey the Blacksmith," the girl says.

Most of her black hair is thick and hangs in heavy waves, but a patch on the side of her head is uneven, bare in some spots. Gauge wonders what caused it. She sees him looking and shifts to hide the patch from view.

The Blacksmith nods a greeting.

"Father, this is . . . I'm sorry," she says, addressing Gauge. "I'm afraid I don't remember your name."

"Gauge," he says, hunching his shoulders. "Gauge the Apprentice, grandson of Bastien the Carpenter." He catches himself. "The late Carpenter."

"May his soul sail in peace," the Blacksmith says.

"Father, Gauge is in something of a bind."

Realizing she knows more than he hoped, the boy tenses, prepares to run.

She continues, "It'd be best if he weren't on the streets at the moment. Do you mind if we keep him a spell?"

"I insist," the Blacksmith says.

Gauge wishes his grandpapá were here with him. The old man was the friendly sort, eager to talk to everyone he met and able to put anyone at ease. But Gauge is entirely unused to any company other than his grandpapá, and being in the presence of strangers—one a girl, no less—has him more than a little flustered. "That's very kind of you," he mumbles, "but I can't stay. I have business to attend to."

"Speak up." The Blacksmith's words are followed by a wet cough.

"I must get to the Wharves," Gauge says only slightly louder.

Roux's gaze falls to his fist, where the mangled feathers—her feathers—stick out. Gauge stiffens, waiting for her accusation.

"Don't be silly," she says, resting an iron teapot on a grate over the fire. "You can't possibly go out there now. You'll be caught and set out to sea within the hour."

The boy knows this, but even so, her words hit him with all the force of a hurricane. Panic causes his eyes to widen, his breathing to become quick and shallow. She's right. He was recognized once today.

A second escape is more than he can hope for. His fingers tighten around the feathers. He can't desert his grandpapá. It's not right, leaving the old man's severed soul to hover over his withering body.

As if she can read his thoughts, Roux crosses the room and rummages in a chest pushed up against the wall. "They'll be looking for a lone boy wearing dark pantaloons and a gray tunic."

She pulls out a pair of cream-colored breeches, a pumpkin-colored tunic, and a worn apron. "Here. Yanis is away visiting family, and they won't be expecting a Blacksmith's Apprentice."

Smoked fish hangs from the eaves. A few potatoes and a bag of grains rest on a simple shelf. A sturdy trestle table dominates the middle of the room, benches on either side. Other than a wooden chest and the chair in which her father sits, two rope beds are the only other furniture. The reward offered by Lord Mayor Vulpine would ease their worry—and the discomfort of the next several winters. "Why are you doing this?" Gauge asks.

The girl tugs at her damaged patch of hair and looks to her father.

"Your grandpapá showed me a great kindness when he sold my little Roux a cane for half its worth," the Blacksmith says.

The boy accepts this explanation.

He doesn't know that the Blacksmith told only half the truth. For he and Roux would have attempted to help Gauge even if the Carpenter had charged them double the cane's worth. Not only because it's the right thing to do, but because the two of them know suffering, know the ache of losing a loved one. Worse, they know the pain of a loved one being falsely accused and set out to sea. They'll do everything they can to stop it from ever happening again.

Chapter Four

You might be happy for Gauge, but I'm not. Not one bit. It's true that Roux seems intent on helping the boy release his grandpapá, but there's also a danger in Gauge becoming attached, in developing a reason to stay, to reject my offer.

You can't possibly understand how much this prospect gets under my skin. It's not only that I'm tired and sore (though that is certainly true), or that I've waited far too long to see my . . . For Wolf's sake, none of this is any of your business. All you need to know is that it's imperative that Gauge take this job—and not only for my sake, or even his (though I'm more certain than ever that this is his best, and perhaps only, option). The fact is, the fate of the entire country rests on his decision. The moment the Release is done, I'll have to make my move.

Gauge knows he should change his clothes quickly, but he can't bring himself to do it. Today, his grand-papá is supposed to be at the market, procuring the supplies they need for the coming week. Tomorrow is the day he and his grandpapá normally haul in water from the barrel outside. After bathing, they put on fresh clothes and use the leftover water to clean what they took off. Somehow, changing clothes on the wrong day feels like a betrayal.

"Are you planning to stand there all day?" Roux asks.

Gauge forces himself to move, transforming from the Carpenter's grandson to a Blacksmith's Apprentice by slipping on the laundered tunic. *If only it were this easy to change who you are,* he thinks. *I'd be free to do as I please.* The sudden hope that flutters inside him is tempered by guilt. *Changing clothes has nothing to do with how much I love my grandpapá,* he reminds himself. *I'm only doing what I must to survive—what Grandpapá would want me to do.*

With a shake of his head, Gauge stuffs the feathers

and the scarf from the Steward into his pocket, intent on setting off for the Wharves as soon as possible. Roux urges him to take a seat at the table.

"You can't leave yet," she says, handing him a bowl of potatoes in a spiced broth. "You should wait until it's nearly dark—not so late that you'll draw attention for being out, but late enough that you won't be as visible as you are by the light of day."

The boy presses his lips together. Sitting here warm and comfortable while his grandpapá's soul is stuck hovering over a lifeless body feels all wrong. His grandpapá needs him. But Gauge won't be able to help his grandpapá at all if he's captured. He imagines Lord Mayor Vulpine's Guards crowding the streets, searching for him. And the reward . . . every villager out there will be eager to claim it.

He doesn't think he'll be able to eat, but his spoon soon scrapes the bottom of the bowl. The food does him some good. For the first time that day, he's able to think clearly.

He replays the events of the last hour, remembers the hatred on Lord Mayor Vulpine's face, the fear that washed through the crowd. Now he understands exactly why his grandpapá hid him away like an ugly scar. He remembers the Steward's accusation.

"What do ravens have to do with anything?" he asks.

After Roux explains, the boy jumps up and paces the room, fuming at the injustice of it all. He tells himself that he had nothing to do with calling me. And the raven appearing, that was nothing more than coincidence. Wasn't it? The boy's doubt grows.

He comforts himself with the knowledge that he would never intentionally call me. That he'd like nothing more than never to see me again.

He remembers the old man's final words, wonders why his grandpapá brought me up after all these winters. The boy's dream comes back to him. The idea of a Wolf stealing a pup out of someone's feet is far too strange to deserve serious contemplation, but his grandpapá used to say that all dreams contain a kernel of truth.

Gauge searches the room, realizes he hasn't seen me since . . .

(At the moment, I'm away fetching another soul. But I wouldn't make an appearance right now anyway—the boy needs his space. Things might be different if the old man hadn't planted a warning about me in the boy's mind before setting sail, but here we are.)

Gauge groans and covers his face with his hands. He let himself believe that I was harmless—that his ability to see me meant nothing. He sees now that he was naïve—that the deaths of Mistress Vulpine and his grandpapá weren't coincidence. He tells himself the villagers were right about me. I'm every bit as dangerous as they said.

Gauge's legs nearly buckle. His life was far from perfect, but he'd give anything for things to go back to the way they were. To go home, to crawl into bed with his grandpapá, to gaze up at the lanterns in the sky. None of that will ever happen again. Grief pierces Gauge's heart like a harpoon. He works to stuff the oozing hole, to shove all his messy feelings back inside.

"I need to go," he says. "The lanterns will soon light."

He expects Roux to argue, but she removes the apron tied at her waist, wraps a shawl about her shoulders, and kisses her father goodbye.

"You're coming with me?"

"If a Guard finds you alone, you're as good as set out to sea."

The boy bristles. He's not a brainless jellyfish—he'll be fine. But there's a part of him that knows she's right. And an even bigger part that is glad not to face what's coming alone.

The Blacksmith grips Roux's hand, squeezes it tenderly. "Smooth sailing, little bird."

Gauge yanks open the door, ignoring the rush of tears that fills his eyes.

Outside, Roux stops to collect the remaining feathers off the line. Gauge shifts uncomfortably, thinking of the ones in his pocket.

"Not a bad knot," she says, nodding at the tree. "Maybe you can show me sometime."

The boy can't help but think that if Lord Mayor Vulpine has his way, there won't be a "sometime" in his future, but he agrees, relieved to be let off the hook.

Moments later, they hurry through nearly empty streets. Warm candles glow behind shuttered windows. A cat mewls in front of one door, which creaks open to grant it admission. Gauge imagines a boy inside the home cradling the cat to his chest, stroking its soft fur. (Actually, the mistress of the house discovered a very large rat helping itself to the roast she prepared. The cat was let in for obvious reasons.)

Gauge keeps his head down but jumps at every sound.

"Relax," Roux hisses. "You look like you're trying to hide something."

"I *am* hiding something," Gauge mutters. He can't possibly relax with all that's happened—as if finding out that he's tied to death isn't bad enough, there's also a price on his head.

Footsteps approach. Gauge tenses as a Guard nears. He's wearing the loose trousers and fitted jacket issued to all Bouge-by-the-Sea Guards. The yellow sash tied around his waist marks his rank (or, more precisely, his loyalty to Lord Mayor Vulpine). He carries a blazing torch in one hand. The other hand rests on the hilt of the sword sheathed at his hip.

But it's the Guard's smell, the sweat mixed with his lye-washed uniform, that gets to Gauge. The last time he came face to face with one of Lord Mayor

Vulpine's Guards was the morning after he shouted about me in front of Mistress Vulpine.

He was in the workshop, sanding a cabinet under Grandpapá's patient tutelage. A burly Guard entered, sword drawn. Grandpapá stepped between the Guard and the boy. "Go wait in our living room," Grandpapá instructed Gauge quietly.

Grandpapá had been acting strangely ever since the boy spotted me the day before, ever since Mistress Vulpine fainted, hitting her head on the counter on the way down. Lord Mayor Vulpine had hurried her from the shop the minute she woke. The old man hadn't let Gauge play outside for the rest of the day and hadn't sent him out for their bread before break-fast the next morning.

"The boy will be coming with me," the Guard said.

"On what grounds?" Grandpapá asked.

"He's been charged with the death of Mistress Vulpine."

Grandpapá gasped. "Mistress Vulpine set sail?"

"Last night. I've been sent for the boy."

"You can't take him," Grandpapá insisted. "He's too young for a trial."

"That's not for you to decide." (In fact, Lord Mayor Vulpine was too absorbed in his grief to care one bit about a trial, regardless of Gauge's age.)

Gauge can't remember much of what came after, though he still recalls the sharp glint of the blade on the Guard's sword as it caught the sun's rays. He wasn't certain what the Guard wanted with him, but he felt the tension in the air and heard the fear in his grandpapá's voice as he begged and pleaded with the Guard.

He remembers Grandpapá emptying his till of shells and fetching all they had stashed in a jar in the back. More than anything, he remembers the threatening look in the Guard's eyes before he departed. "If word of this gets back to Lord Mayor Vulpine, both you and the boy will find yourselves set out to sea."

Then the Guard left. Gauge's grandpapá sank down on his knees, clutching Gauge in a terrified embrace. After that, everything changed.

"You there," the Guard in front of him says, interrupting Gauge's memories.

Gauge freezes.

"Good evening," Roux says pleasantly. "Can we help you?"

"What are you two doing out and about this time of day?"

"We're . . . going down to the sea. To collect feathers. The Steward has put in a large order and I'm running low." Roux motions to her bulging pockets. Luckily, the Guard doesn't look too closely. He's busy peering at Gauge.

"We're looking for a missing boy, a Voyant."

Gauge swallows and forces himself to meet the Guard's piercing gaze. The man's eyes are deep set, drawing attention to his thick, bushy brows.

"What does he look like?" Roux's voice is innocent, but her hand reaches for her hair. She wraps a strand tightly around her finger.

"About this high—" The Guard holds up a hand to Gauge's height. His eyes narrow. "Skinny. Dark hair. Wearing brown pantaloons and a gray tunic."

"Haven't seen anyone like that," Roux says.

"What's your name?" the Guard asks Gauge.

"My name?" Gauge asks.

Roux answers. "He's my father's Apprentice."

"I asked his name."

Gauge looks around. A vendor is packing up his cart of smoked eel. "Eel," Gauge blurts.

"Eel?" The Guard lifts an eyebrow.

"Not Eel," Gauge says, his brain spinning. "Eli."

"Don't think I've seen you before. You from around here, *Eli*?"

Gauge can't think of anything to say that won't give him away.

"He's from Montpeyroux,"[5] Roux says smoothly. "He's not the sharpest hook on the line, but my father says what he lacks in brains, he makes up for with his hard work."

The Guard inspects Gauge's clothing. Gauge hides his unblemished hands behind his back.

"Bit scrawny for a Blacksmith's Apprentice, aren't you?" the Guard asks.

"Father says he's strong as an ox," Roux says.

The Guard lets out a disbelieving harrumph. Gauge tenses, ready to run.

"If you do see the boy, take care," the Guard finally says. "He could be dangerous."

---

5. *It's MAHN-puh-roo.*

Swallowing his stunned laughter, Gauge nods in what he hopes is an agreeable manner.

"Thank you, sir." Roux grips Gauge's arm and pulls him past the Guard.

After they round the corner, she leans against a stone wall and presses a hand to her chest. "That was a close one."

Gauge is too frightened to relax.

Roux giggles nervously. "Eel?"

Gauge glares. "Not the sharpest hook on the line?"

She shrugs. "It worked, didn't it?"

Gauge can't argue. "Why did you tell him I was from Montpeyroux?"

"It was the first thing I thought of." Roux resumes walking and adds in a softer voice, "My mother grew up there."

Montpeyroux is one of the neighboring countries Gauge's grandpapá told stories about. Outside of Gatineau's borders, things like birth and death operate by a completely different set of rules. Gauge strains to remember what he knows of the country. "That's the place where babies are grown in crops like cabbage, right?"

Roux nods. "Mother said rabbits deliver the babies to their families."

Gauge wonders if Roux was grown in a crop but figures it would be rude to ask. "Where is your mother?"

"She set sail." Roux's teeth clamp together. She tugs on her hair.

Gauge can't help but think there's something she's not telling him. His chest tightens. It's as if death is surrounding him, pressing in on all sides. His legs threaten to buckle, but he has to keep going—for his grandpapá's sake.

The square is empty save two maidens perched on a stone bench, hands clasped, heads bent together, whispering conspiratorially. They glance his way, then return to their conversation. Are they talking about him? Calling him a Voyant? Gauge clenches his jaw and lengthens his stride. So what if he can see the stupid Wolf?

He wants to believe that, but deep down he knows that if it really didn't matter, his grandpapá wouldn't have kept him hidden. He swallows the bitter lump of shame in his throat, hating how his emotions, normally smooth and steady, now flap like sails on a boat changing directions with the wind.

In the distance, the Wharves come into view. Two figures stand at attention, illuminated by flickering torches. Gauge skids to a stop. "Guards."

Roux slaps her forehead. "We should have known."

She turns toward home, but an idea glimmers in the back of the boy's mind. It's a wild one, a dangerous one, but he isn't ready to give up—can't give up. "Follow me."

He leads her north, away from the sea, and then he veers west until they arrive back at the cliffs, this time above the port. A pulley system runs beside them with carts to transport seafood and other supplies up and down the cliff, but it's shut down for the day.

He starts down the steep staircase.

"I don't understand," Roux says. "The Wharves are up here." Her brows draw together as though she thinks he might not be working with a full set of tools.

"Trust me," Gauge says, feigning confidence.

A memory floods Gauge, blurring his vision. The

last time he was on these steps was shortly before the incident with Mistress Vulpine. His grandpapá closed the shop early one evening and took him clamming. The old man taught Gauge how to dig their shells from the sand, how to clean and shuck them. They cooked the clams in goat milk and enjoyed a delicious stew.

Gauge blinks and focuses on the staircase, which is slick with trickling meltwater.

They carefully descend all two hundred and seventy-two steps. (Roux counted once. Actually, she counted twice because she thought she might have made a mistake, but it turns out she was right the first time.)

Finally, they step onto a silent dock brimming with fishing boats tied up for the night. Several larger ships bob farther out in the bay, waves lapping at their sides. Storage shacks crouch under the cliff's edge. On their left, a beach gives way to rocky tidepools. At the end of the beach, the peninsula holding the Wharves juts into the water, its cliff silhouetted against the gauzy evening sky. Lazy waves lap at the shore, irritating Gauge with their nonchalance.

A hairy, sun-ripened Guard steps out from the shadows of the cliff, his wild, rust-colored beard bobbing as he speaks. Behind him, a blazing torch is mounted on the sheer rock wall. "Your business?"

Gauge freezes. He should have expected another Guard. He can't think, can't move. *Dan-ger, Dan-ger,* his heart thumps.

"Evening," Roux says smoothly. "We're here to collect feathers."

"In the dark?"

"We have a little time yet. Besides, they're all over the tide pools. Hardly need any light at all to find them." (This is a stretch—there aren't that many feathers to be found. Luckily, the Guard has seen Roux collecting feathers around the village and believes her story.)

"Very well," the Guard says, adjusting his yellow sash. "But keep an eye out. There's a Voyant on the loose."

"We heard," Roux says. "Any reports on where he might be?"

Roux's dark eyes flash at the Guard. He's a foot taller than her and several winters older, but she doesn't cower, holds herself as an equal. The boy tries to imagine having that much confidence but can only see himself running for the stairs.

"Nothing yet," the Guard says. "It's like he vanished into thin air."

"We'll let you know if we see anything." Roux turns to Gauge. "Come on. Let's get to work."

As they walk away, the sand swallows Gauge's shoes, causing him to stumble. "What's with all the torches?"

Roux thinks he might be joking, but seeing he's not, she answers. "To keep the Wolf away. Now look like you're searching."

The boy follows Roux's lead, stooping to collect feathers for her collection. With each one he picks up, he feels lighter, more hopeful. By the time they near the end of the beach, his hands and pockets are stuffed with all the feathers he needs to release his grandpapá *and* repay Roux. A small mound of rocks forms a wall in front of them. They scramble over the pile, relieved that the outcropping provides a screen from the Guard's prying eyes. Roux grabs Gauge's hand and urges him to run.

They slow and she drops his hand. He feels the absence, rubs his thumb over his palm, notes the warmth left over from her touch.

(This is a terribly upsetting development. Forming attachments will only lead to heartbreak for Gauge. Besides, it's entirely unnecessary. Look at me—I've been a Wolf for centuries and I'm doing fine without a single acquaintance, thank you very much.)

As they reach the cliff, Roux spins toward him. "What's next?"

Gauge's grandpapá never let him past the fence on the unstable tip of the cliff, but he claimed there was an old, crumbling staircase carved right through the rock.

The boy studies the rock and lets out a loud sigh of relief. He leads Roux to a spot where water has whittled away the stone. It hangs out over the sea, leaving a small, exposed cavern. He peels off his shoes, relishing the gritty sand under the soft soles of his bare feet.

The chilly water bites at his ankles. He draws in a sharp breath.

Roux splashes behind him.

Inside, their eyes strain to make sense of the dark.

"Help me find an opening," Gauge says.

They stretch out their hands, careful not to drop their shoes as they feel along the damp, jagged walls.

"Here," Roux calls. "I found it!"

A narrow gap reveals a staircase carved into the cliff. The two work their way upward, moving slowly and methodically.

"Is this safe?" Roux asks.

Gauge shrugs. "I doubt it."

"How did you find this?" Roux asks. "Who put it here?"

"My grandpapá told me it was built as an escape route in case the village was ever under siege. At one point, Lord Mayors probably kept boats in the cavern."

(His grandpapá was a boy the last time a neighboring country dared attack.)

Their calves burn as they climb the spiral staircase, winding up through a dark shaft with slimy walls before finally emerging into the fresh night air on the point of the cliff, greeted by the same rickety fence the boy remembers seeing from the other side. For a moment, he's caught up in memories of running around the Wharves, stretching his legs as the wind chased after him.

Roux gasps. "Look."

Gauge turns around and lets out a gasp of his own. One wrong step and he and Roux will both plunge to the sea far below. But it isn't only the danger that captures his attention. The water stretches out in front of them like a shimmering mirror. A sliver of moon hovers on the horizon and thousands—millions—of lights blink high overhead, the lanterns of sailors navigating the Sea-in-the-Sky.

The boy stands mesmerized, drinking in the sight. His mother is up there somewhere, the light from her houseboat shining down on him. Soon, his grandpapá will join her. (Even if the boy's beliefs about the Sea-in-the-Sky are nonsense, I understand his longing. I can almost feel my daughter throw herself into my arms and bury her face in my neck. For a moment, I smell her sweet, milk-scented breath.)

"Let's go," the boy finally says. They slip on their shoes.

Gauge straightens.

"Stay down," Roux whispers, tugging at him. They peer over the fence, scanning the Wharves. I'm tucked in the shadow of the chestnut tree. Two Guards stand at attention at the Wharves' front gate, their backs turned. One wrong move and the boy will be set out to sea for sure. They both will.

The children lower themselves to their bellies and slide carefully under the wooden fence, ignoring the ground's icy chill. Crouching on the other side, they tiptoe closer to the old man's hole. The sight of his grandpapá's form laid out in the vessel is nearly more than Gauge can bear. He falls to his knees and buries his face in the old man's chest.

"I did it, Grandpapá," he sobs. "I brought feathers to complete your Release."

"Shhh," Roux warns.

Gauge knows he needs to distribute the feathers around his grandpapá's vessel, but now that he's here, he can't make himself do it. Once the old man has the feathers, there will be nothing holding him down, nothing keeping him nearby. The thought makes Gauge feel empty and untethered, as if he could float right up into the sky and light a lantern of his own.

Roux remains silent as long as she is able. "Gauge," she finally whispers, "we can't stay here forever."

She jerks her chin toward the Guards at the front gate. Then she adds, "The Guard down below will grow suspicious if we don't return."

The boy lifts his head, wipes his eyes. She's right. He has to do this. For his grandpapá.

With great care, he smooths each of the feathers one by one and tucks them inside the old man's vessel. Without a word, Roux moves closer. Pulling more feathers from her pockets, she joins Gauge, adorning the boat with the best of her lot.

When the two finish, the only sound is their breathing.

"It's time," Roux finally says.

Gauge wishes he could bury his grandpapá's body, but he knows he's done what he can, what really matters. He leans over and kisses the old man's cold cheek. "Sail in peace, Grandpapá," he whispers.

He rises and creeps toward the fence, unable to look back.

Despite the grief weighing his every step, the smallest bit of hope glimmers deep underneath his suffering—now that his grandpapá is gone, the boy thinks that maybe I'll finally leave him alone.

The children's silhouettes move closer to the edge of the cliff. I watch them go, wishing I could hurry them along. But they'll slide under the fence and make their way down the stairs soon enough. When they finally reach the beach, I'll be waiting.

Chapter Five

Gauge and Roux emerge from the cavern, slip into their shoes, and pick their way along the beach. Gauge doesn't notice me at first—he's too caught up in his pain, in his suffering. It's my smell that finally alerts him. He sniffs and then peers into the dark.

I step closer, letting the moon bathe me in a glow of pale light.

"You," he says.

Right away, I see that I've made a mistake. Rage burns in the boy's eyes. Accusations. Hatred. My appearance has ripped the newly formed scab off his aching heart, exposing the raw wounds underneath. He blames me. For the winters he spent cowering in the back of his grandpapá's workshop. For taking away the one person who loved him. Whom he loved in return.

"Please, listen," I say.

Gauge is stunned to hear me speak. "You . . . you can talk?"

"That's not important now. I need to tell you—"

The boy clenches his fists. "How dare you!"

"It's not what you think." I mean for this to be reassuring, but it comes out as a growl.

"What is it?" Roux asks. "Who are you talking to?" She stops walking and peers into the dark.

"It's the Great White Wolf," Gauge says. "It's here. In front of us."

Roux's hand flies to her mouth. Her eyes dart from side to side, searching out an escape.

"What?" Gauge asks me, his anger building. "My grandpapá wasn't enough? Now you've come for me, too?"

"That's not—"

"You think you're so clever, sneaking around, watching my every move. But I've known you were here since the beginning. And now I've released my grandpapá and there isn't anything you can do to me that will hurt more than losing him. So go ahead. Take me."

(It isn't true, of course—the boy had no idea I was here. And despite his misery, he has no wish to set sail. But he's itching for a fight, too angry to think through his words.)

A crab scuttles over his foot.

"I'm not here to take you."

"You're not?" The boy stumbles backward.

"What's going on?" Roux asks, steadying him.

Gauge shakes his head.

"I have an offer for you," I say. "A proposition. Something that can help us both."

"An offer." Gauge is incredulous.

"I'm here to help."

At this, the boy's anger flares. "Help, like you did killing Mistress Vulpine? My grandpapá? Who is it next—her?"

He waves a hand Roux's direction. She cringes.

"It's not like that," I say. "I don't kill anyone. I don't have that power."

The boy remembers his grandpapá's warning. *Stay away from the Wolf.* He steps back. "I want you to go away, to stop following me. Leave me alone. Do you hear? Leave *us* alone."

"Wait," I say, silently cursing the Carpenter. "Let me—"

Gauge grabs Roux's hand. They lunge around me, scramble over the tide pools, and sprint across the beach, slowing down when they near the stairs so as not to raise suspicion with the Guard.

I long to flop down and let the gritty sand dig into my skin, let the waves wash over me.

This boy is my only hope. Truthfully, he's the only hope for all of Gatineau. Not even magic lasts forever, and my increasing aches and pains tell me the end is drawing near. If I set sail without a replacement, I (and everyone who sets sail forever after) will be left to fester. We'll be stuck with our decaying bodies until we sink slowly to the Bog, where we'll be trapped for all eternity.

A low growl rumbles deep in my throat. I'd hoped that with the old man out of the way, the boy would have nothing to lose and everything to gain. But I can't force him to take the job. I can't even compel him to hear me out. I'm going to have to lie low and bide my time. Wait until his emotions aren't burning quite so hot and he's willing to listen to reason. There's a chance that he will adjust to his new life, that he will form new bonds, new attachments. But what choice do I have?

Roux is shaking as they scale the top of the stairs and move quickly through the dimly lit streets, their only light the lanterns flickering high above.

"What did the Wolf want?" she finally asks.

Everything the boy has endured swells inside him, a wave threatening to pull him under. He tells her about me, Mistress Vulpine, his five-winter exile, even his dream.

Roux is a practical sort. While she was raised according to Gatineau's customs, her mother shared enough of her own beliefs with both her husband and daughter to open their minds to other possibilities.

This puts Roux in the position of being one of the few people in all the country who might accept Gauge's story. Or at least acknowledge the possibility that it could be true. Now that the initial shock has passed, Roux is more curious than frightened.

"What did it look like?"

The boy shrugs. "A Wolf."

Roux nudges him, silently asking for more details.

"White hair. A bit mangy, truth be told."

(I'm incredibly embarrassed by this assessment, but I can't deny it.)

"Tell me again what it said?"

"She," Gauge says.

"Excuse me?"

"The Wolf is a girl."

Roux doesn't know what to make of this news. "Well, what did *she* say?"

Gauge walks her through the conversation.

"What do you think her proposition was?"

"Don't know, don't care," Gauge says. "I only want her to leave me alone."

"Why can you see her and no one else?"

The boy has been asking himself that very thing. (And he has yet to figure out why his grandpapá warned him about a Wolf that the old man couldn't have known was still around.)

Roux adjusts her shawl as their footfalls echo on the empty street. "Now that you've sent her away, do you think, well . . . are you worried you've upset her? What if she comes for you next?"

The boy narrows his eyes. "Let her try."

Roux doesn't doubt his determination, but she questions how one lone boy could possibly fend off the Wolf. As they hurry home, she glances over her shoulder, half-expecting to find me lurking behind them. (I'm not. My territory covers all of Gatineau. At present, I'm fetching a soul far out in the country—a sickly old woman ready for her journey. Not that Roux could see me even if I were behind them.)

As they turn a corner, they see a group of Guards moving down the street, torches in hand. Roux yanks Gauge out of sight. "They're searching for you," she says. "They must be."

The two retrace their steps, adding distance to their trip in an effort to avoid the groups of Guards that seem to appear on nearly every corner.

When they finally arrive back at the smithy, the Blacksmith's face lights up. "It's done, then?"

"It is, Father." She bends and kisses him, noting the tired rings around his eyes, his rattling breath. "How are you feeling?"

"No better, no worse," the Blacksmith says. It's not entirely true. A new tightness has taken over his chest, making each breath more difficult than the previous one. Still, he feels he has time, that he may turn a corner. There's no need to worry his daughter, not yet.

Roux stokes the fire, intent on boiling water for a pot of tea. Gauge hovers in the doorway, repeatedly checking over his shoulder to see if I followed him.

He reaches for his pocket, but his knife isn't there. He searches his mind, remembers leaving it under his pillow. He bites the inside of his cheek, drawing blood.

"Are you going to stand there all night?" Roux asks. "Sit, warm yourself."

She points to the hearth.

Soon, the boy is situated in front of the fire with a steaming cup of dandelion tea, which warms first his hands and then his belly. As he drinks, his gaze keeps darting back to the door. He can't help but think that if I found him before, I might do so again. He wonders what I wanted from him. Then he shoves the thought away. He doesn't care what I want—he's not about to strike up a deal with—with what? He doesn't know what to call me. Death?

He shakes his head, amazed at such ludicrous thoughts. He tells himself that I am a killer—no more, no less. He realizes that if Roux is right—if he provoked me into attacking—he's going to need something with which to defend himself. He needs his knife.

(Please, allow me to set the record straight. I could no sooner hurt him than I could sprout a second head. In the very beginning, before I realized that I didn't need to eat, I chased down a rabbit. I caught it, but then something compelled me to let it go. I don't know if it's a blessing or a curse, but I've learned over the winters that I can't harm any living creature. That said, the boy's knife would tear at my body the same as it would anyone else's.)

Roux pulls a feather mattress out from under a bed in the corner and drags it to the front of the fire. "I'm sure Yanis won't mind."

Outside, dogs bark and howl, no doubt disturbed by the Guards searching every alley. The boy knows that he should argue. His very presence puts Roux and her father at risk. It's bad enough that Lord Mayor Vulpine is after him. The last thing they need is a murderous Wolf paying them a visit.

But the day's events have left him with little choice and even less energy. He rests his empty mug on the hearth and sinks into the blanket's warm embrace. He doesn't let himself fall into sleep. After Roux and the Blacksmith are in bed, their breaths coming in regular puffs, he quietly, gingerly, slips from under the blanket and makes his way across the room.

His fingers ache as he grips the cooking knife's unfamiliar handle. He longs for his folding knife, imagines pressing the blade against a hunk of wood, imagines stripping away first its bark and then the fibers underneath, shaping the raw form into something it never knew it could become.

This knife is big and clumsy. No good for carving and probably not much help against a Wolf, if he's being honest. But at least it's something.

The boy isn't yet ready for sleep. Clutching the knife, he slips outside, shivering when the chilly air nips at his skin. The Sea-in-the-Sky is lit with more lanterns than he can count. He scans them, hoping his grandpapá's will somehow stand out.

"Where are you, Grandpapá?" he whispers. The lanterns twinkle. The boy comforts himself with the thought that the journey must take some time. His grandpapá is probably still traveling.

Gauge lowers his head and slips back inside, where he stashes the knife under his pillow. Even there it feels wrong—too big, too different.

He knows his grandpapá's shop is probably being guarded for his possible return, but he vows to find a way to fetch his folding knife the next day. After he has that, his one small reminder of his previous life, he'll have to find a way out of the village. Before Lord Mayor Vulpine's Guards find him.

I only developed a taste for mornings after I had Émilie. Then I started slipping from bed a few minutes before the sun peeked over the horizon, enjoying a quiet spell by the fire before plunging into the chaos that daylight brings. Roux, on the other hand, has always been a morning person.

As the first embers of dawn smolder outside the window, she springs from bed and fetches water from the barrel out back, breaking the icy surface and filling her bucket. Back inside, she splashes her face, wraps a scarf around her neck to fight off a chill, and takes in

Gauge's sleeping form. Her heart aches for what he's endured, for what is sure to come. But she is a practical girl and knows sitting around moping won't do.

She pokes the boy awake. "Out of the way," she says. "Unless you'd like to go hungry."

He jumps up, disoriented. In the corner, the Blacksmith tosses and turns on his rope bed as he snores unevenly. The previous day crashes down on the boy, buckling his legs and blurring his eyes. He hopes Roux doesn't notice as he swipes at his face.

"There's wood out back," she says, blowing on the embers in the hearth. "Make yourself useful and fetch me a load."

Gauge slips the cooking knife back on the table before following her orders. He hasn't forgotten his decision to fetch his folding knife, but he's grateful for an easier task to begin the day.

The chilly air causes goose bumps to rise on his arms. He enjoys the cold. It's a reminder that, at least for the moment, he's alive.

A mouse scurries out from under a log, squeaking with alarm.

Gauge kicks the stack of wood. "Perfect," he

mutters. "Even the mice are scared of me."

He loads five split logs into his arms. Their sharp corners and splintered edges press into his skin.

"That'll do for now," Roux says after he carries them inside and stacks them beside the hearth. "Fill the pot with water, won't you?"

The blade of the cooking knife gleams as she uses it to chop beets and an onion.

Gauge hurries to do her bidding. He's not sure what he did to deserve this kindness, why they haven't kicked him out. (It's a fair question. History has shown over and over that not just anyone will risk their life to help a perfect stranger.) For a fleeting moment, he lets himself imagine what it would be like to stay, to become part of a family again. He reminds himself that such thoughts are useless and turns his attention to the matter of retrieving his knife.

With a little luck, there will only be a single Guard posted at the front door. Gauge's hand clenches as though it already holds the folding knife. Deep down, he knows it won't be any more use against me than any other blade. But the knife is more than a weapon. Now that his grandpapá is gone, it's a prized possession. The one thing he can claim as his own. He'll need it for self-defense, to pass time; perhaps it'll even help him earn a living—if nothing else, he can sell carvings. More importantly, with the folding knife in his pocket, he'll be carrying a little bit of his grandpapá wherever he goes.

When the beets are boiling, Roux takes the lid off a ceramic pot tucked on a shelf. The smell of vinegar floods the room. She chops up a mackerel and adds it to the soup.

"It'll be on the thin side," she says, "but we'll manage."

Gauge hardly hears her. He's caught up in memories of his grandpapá's last night, when he promised himself he'd learn the old man's favorite fish. Could it be mackerel? Countless times they fixed it, fried it, boiled it—did the old man ever say anything about it being his favorite?

The boy can't recall a single image of his grandpapá lifting a bite to his mouth. Gauge's breaths come in heavy puffs as his mind tumbles frantically through time, trying to find some memory to hold on to. Finally, he lands on something. It's not an image of his grandpapá eating but of the old man teaching him to fillet a fish. It was Gauge's first time and he flipped open his folding knife, eager to make his grandpapá proud. He cringed as the old man showed him how to slice behind the gills on either side, cutting off the head.

But he did it. After he freed the fillet, they roasted it over the fire and enjoyed the bold taste. Gauge squeezes his eyes shut, searching the memory. As hard as he tries, he can't remember his grandpapá saying it was his favorite. But he recalls the approval on the old man's face as Gauge finished preparing the fish and carried it to the fire. "Well done, my boy," his grandpapá said.

As the fish sizzled in the pan, a bell rang from the shop. His grandpapá's smile disappeared, his mouth pinched tight. While the old man rushed into the store, Gauge stayed in the back, wishing he could do something to make his grandpapá proud not only in private but also out in the open for all the world to see.

Now the Blacksmith rolls over and pushes himself up to sitting. Roux perches at her father's side. "How are you this morning?" she asks, grabbing his hand.

A shadow crosses the Blacksmith's face. "Help me

to the table," he says. "Nothing wrong with me a bit of your soup won't fix."

"It's nothing like Mother's," Roux says, but her shoulders straighten as she helps the Blacksmith to his feet. After he's settled, Roux dishes him a bowl of soup. The Blacksmith's hand, scarred from a lifetime of working with blazing metal, shakes as he lifts his spoon. Gauge notices that he sips the broth, avoiding the chunks of fish and vegetables.

The boy has no such reservations. Although thin, the soup is richly spiced. Gauge tastes parsley, chives, and something else he can't quite name. His forehead wrinkles. "Is that chervil?"

"How did you know?" Roux asks, grinning delightedly.

"My grandpapá loved to cook," Gauge says, squeezing his spoon tightly. Even when food was scarce, the old man always tried to add a little seasoning to their pot. He taught Gauge how a pinch of rosemary could improve the taste of potatoes, a bit of thyme could transform an otherwise forgettable soup, and mint went with almost any fish.

Gauge briefly closes his eyes and pretends his grandpapá is sitting across the table.

"It must be very hard without him," Roux says.

Gauge doesn't answer. Can't answer. He's like the carcass of a long-dead insect, ready to crumble at the slightest provocation.

All too soon, his bowl is empty.

"I'm sorry we can't offer another helping," Roux says. "We need this pot to stretch through dinner."

"I'm stuffed," the boy says, setting down his spoon.

His stomach growls, betraying his words.

"Father will soon be back at work. Once the shop is open again, we'll eat better than Lord Mayor Vulpine himself. Isn't that right, Father?"

"Take this," her father says, passing his bowl to Gauge while avoiding his daughter's eyes.

(Typical. Rather than deal with the hard truths, you humans often sweep them under the ashes, hoping to spare your loved ones pain. Not that I can throw dead fish; I used to do exactly the same thing.)

The Blacksmith continues, "I've had my fill."

Roux frowns as she takes in her father's half-eaten meal. "I'll save it for later. When you've built up more of an appetite."

"Give it to the boy."

"But Father——"

"No, I can't——" Gauge says.

"Do as I say." The Blacksmith's voice allows no argument.

Roux's chin trembles as she dumps her father's soup into Gauge's bowl. The boy doesn't move.

"Go on, eat up," the Blacksmith urges. "No sense in wasting good food."

Gauge lifts the spoon to his mouth. With each bite, he can't help but feel that he's stealing a bit of the Blacksmith's life. After a few mouthfuls, Gauge pushes back his bowl. "I couldn't eat another bite."

"I insist."

Gauge bites his lower lip, unable to look the Blacksmith in the eye.

"Tell me your story," the Blacksmith says.

Gauge isn't interested in telling his story again. His wounds are too raw, too recent.

"Come, my boy. Surely, we deserve to know what we are up against."

Gauge's head snaps up. *We?*

(At this, my stomach lurches violently. I do believe all the stress is giving me an ulcer.)

In the face of the Blacksmith's kindness, Gauge owes the man an explanation.

"They say I'm a Voyant." He's amazed at how easily the word rolls off his tongue.

"I suspected as much. Are you?"

Gauge studies the rough-hewn planks on the floor. "There is a Wolf. But I don't command it. And I'm not from the Bog. I swear it on all the fish in the sea."

The Blacksmith sees that the boy is earnest.

He doesn't know what business the boy and I have with each other, but he can't bring himself to believe the child sitting in front of him is dangerous.

"Father," Roux says carefully. "I'd like to invite Gauge to stay with us until Yanis returns."

"Our doors will remain open for as long as he needs a safe harbor," the Blacksmith says firmly.

Roux lowers her spoon. Her eyebrows stitch together, showing her worry. "But Father," she says, preparing to argue, "once Yanis returns—"

A coughing spell overtakes the Blacksmith. When it ends, he says, "Change is made in small increments, one right action at a time."

Roux adjusts the scarf around her neck. It's the

color of a blazing sunset and makes her eyes seem even darker and more luminous than usual (a fact that is not lost on Gauge).

"What will we do when Yanis returns?" she asks.

"We'll cross that isthmus when we get to it," the Blacksmith says.

"I can't stay," Gauge says.

"Where do you mean to go?" The Blacksmith leans forward.

"I don't know, but I'll never be safe here, not as long as Lord Mayor Vulpine is in power."

The Blacksmith rubs his temples. "There's a ship leaving in four days. I know the Captain."

(Four days? That doesn't give me much time. Once the boy is on that ship, once he crosses Gatineau's border, I won't be able to reach him.)

Gauge attempts to swallow. Traveling outside of Bouge is one thing. Living in a new country—that's something he never imagined. His heart twangs as he thinks of the comfortable life he lived with his grand-papá. But this ship could be his only chance. "I don't have anything to offer for payment."

"The Captain owes me a favor," the Blacksmith

says. "For now, we need a place to keep you safely hidden."

"I thought you said he could stay here?" Roux asks.

Banging sounds from somewhere down the street. A dog barks a warning.

"I don't imagine Lord Mayor Vulpine is going to leave a single stone unturned," the Blacksmith says. "You can bet your last lure that noise we hear is his men searching every building in the village."

Gauge flinches. He's used to hovering in the shadows, unseen by all but his grandpapá. Now, the old man is dead, and Gauge is being hunted by Lord Mayor Vulpine *and* the Great White Wolf. Like a rat on a sinking ship, he's running out of places to hide. If he's to survive, he'll have to fight. For that, he needs his knife.

(For the love of all the sharks in the sea, why must humans always assume violence is the answer?)

The noise down the street moves closer. A shiver runs down Gauge's back.

Run, Gauge hears his grandpapá whisper. *Run, and don't come back.*

Chapter Six

Roux rushes into the shop. Gauge reluctantly follows.

She peeks out a window. "Father was right. It's the Guards."

Gauge's first thought is to flee out the back. But Lord Mayor Vulpine isn't one to do things quietly—where there is one Guard, there are sure to be many more. The boy won't make it beyond the alley.

It's been several summers since he played Hide and Seek and he's quite out of practice. There doesn't seem to be anywhere to hide in the small shop, which contains only metal, tools, and items waiting for repair.

Luckily, Roux played Hide and Seek as recently as the previous summer. What's more, she knows all the best places.

"In there," she says, pointing to the brick forge. "Hurry!"

The enormous knee-high hearth is open to the room. "They'll see me first thing!"

"Not up there—underneath, by the tuyere."

Gauge lunges for the small opening under the hearth, determined to squeeze inside. The fit is tight, hardly larger than his shoulders. (It's ingenious, I'll give them that. I've seen toddlers crawl in these spaces before—one who fell asleep without his mother knowing, nearly scaring the poor woman half to death when she couldn't find him—but never half-grown boys.)

Gauge is stuck on his side, his body curled around a tube designed to channel air to the hearth above. He pulls his feet in as a Guard pounds on the door.

"Open up," a rough voice yells. "By order of Lord Mayor Vulpine."

Roux straightens her shoulders and swings the door open. "What is it?" she asks.

An ill-tempered Guard (who only recently passed from his youth into manhood and is drunk on his newfound power) brushes her aside and enters. "We have orders to search every dwelling in the village."

"Don't tell me you are still looking for the Voyant?" Roux asks.

"We are."

"Oh dear." Roux fiddles with her apron, feigning concern.

The Guard pokes around the shop, using his torch to light the shadowed corners. "No need to trouble yourself. We'll round him up soon enough."

"Who is it?" the Blacksmith calls from the other room.

"Don't worry, Father. It's only Lord Mayor Vulpine's Guards, searching for the Voyant."

"Let's hope they make short work of it," the Blacksmith calls back. "We can't have that kind of trouble on the loose in Bouge."

The Guard approaches the hearth.

Gauge holds his breath. Something tickles inside his ear. He's certain it's a spider, but he doesn't dare move.

The Guard leans inside the hearth and peers upward, checking the chimney.

Roux steps forward. "Perhaps you'd like to inspect the back?"

Gauge's right calf cramps. He writhes but presses his lips together to prevent any sound from escaping.

The Guard hesitates and then follows Roux to the living room. His gaze lands on the table. His pimpled forehead furrows. "Three bowls?"

Roux and her father share a glance. "Our Apprentice," Roux says.

"And where is this Apprentice of yours?"

"He left straightaway after eating. He's visiting his family in Nimes while Father recovers."

As if on cue, a coughing fit overtakes the Blacksmith.

"Nimes," the Guard says suspiciously. "Surely, this Apprentice would have needed a full meal for such a long journey. Yet his bowl is only half-empty."

"That was his second," Roux explains. She feels certain the Guard knows she's lying, but she's determined not to let him slip her up.

"And how is it that his bowl is yet to be cleared from the table?"

Again the Blacksmith coughs. "I've been busy

nursing my father," Roux explains. "A great many chores have had to wait."

The Guard squints, thinking. "Very well," he finally says. "I shall leave you to your peace. But know this: anyone caught harboring the Voyant will be set out to sea by the day's end."

"As they should be," Roux says.

Meanwhile, Gauge's cramp has passed, leaving behind an aching muscle. He waits for the Guard's footsteps to cross the shop and disappear. The front door closes and Roux leans up against it, relief draining what's left of her energy. "It's clear," she says. "You can come out."

That proves a great deal more complicated than going in. Gauge wiggles and squirms until he's maneuvered himself back into the open room, and then he digs at his ear, chasing out the offending spider.

"Come." Roux glances fearfully at the nearest window. "Let's get you into the back."

The boy follows, his legs shaking so hard it's a miracle they can carry his weight. He can't stop thinking about the way that other Guard's sword glinted in the light back when he came for Gauge all those winters ago. Gauge was scared then, but he was too young to fully understand what was happening. He was scared because his grandpapá—who never feared anything—was scared.

Gauge reaches again for the knife he doesn't have.

Roux shuts the living room door, cutting them off from the shop. "That was close."

"I owe you—" Gauge begins, his voice shaking.

"You owe us nothing," the Blacksmith says. "And I'll hear no further talk otherwise. Now help me to bed. All the excitement has worn me out."

Gauge and Roux both hurry to the Blacksmith's side.

Soon, his snores fill the room.

The cooking knife glints from its spot at the table.

"I must be going," Gauge says at the exact same moment Roux says, "I owe you an apology."

"An apology for what?"

"Go where?"

They share a small smile. "Sorry," Gauge says. His stomach flutters like wood shavings caught in the wind. "Please, continue."

"I'm sorry," Roux says. She tangles her fingers in her curls.

"For what?"

She sinks down at the table. "For making it seem as though you weren't welcome to stay earlier. It's only that my father is so sick, and truthfully, he doesn't seem to be recovering. It'll almost certainly be another two or three days before Yanis returns and we're running low on provisions."

Gauge swallows. He's responsible for their dwindling food supply and can't help but think of the danger he's putting Roux and her father in.

The Blacksmith groans and rolls over. Roux's face darkens. "I suspect he's more ill than he's letting on."

The boy wants to offer the reassurance she's looking for, but he can't come up with anything to say. He dumps what's left of the soup back in the cooking pot, wipes his bowl clean, and then carries it to the storage shelf.

Roux clears her throat. "Do you think I might ask you for a favor?"

She pulls out a few strands of her hair.

Gauge waits for her to cringe from the pain, but

she seems to find the habit soothing, like the comfort he takes in flicking his folding knife open and closed.

"The Steward will be expecting another batch of feathers, but I don't dare leave Father alone."

The very thought of the Steward leaves the taste of rotten fish in the boy's mouth. "How long will you be gone?"

"I'll return midafternoon."

Now that Gauge has his mind set on retrieving his knife, he can't bear the thought of putting it off. He searches for an excuse. "What if the Guards return?"

"You know where to hide."

Gauge shivers, unsure if it's from the idea of stuffing himself back in the cramped space under the hearth or the idea of the Guard coming back. But he can't deny her request—not after all she's done for him.

She sees the acceptance on his face and springs from the bench. "Be sure you keep track of the fire. And offer him a bit of tea when he wakes. I'll be . . ."

She continues issuing instructions. Gauge clenches his jaw, irritated that she's treating him like a child.

As she opens the door, he remembers his debt and springs from his chair.

"Here," he says, pulling the last of his feathers from his pockets.

She opens her mouth.

"I'm not a thief," he says. "I don't normally—"

"I would have done the same," she says, accepting the feathers. The door closes behind her. Silence curls around the boy, and he sinks down at the table. His head falls into his hands. What he'd give to talk to his grandpapá, to feel the old man's strong hand rest on his shoulder.

You're a good boy, his grandpapá always said.

He tried to be. He worked hard to please the old man in the shop and in the evenings. Now the comfort of their quiet, organized life is gone. He reminds himself that even if he retrieves his knife—even if he survives the Wolf—there is still Lord Mayor Vulpine to contend with.

"Help me, Grandpapá," Gauge whispers. "I don't know what to do."

His grandpapá's oft-repeated advice comes to him: *Follow your heart. It's as true as any compass out there.*

Gauge straightens. For now, his heart is telling him to do what he must to survive. He slips his hand in his pocket. He'll retrieve his knife as soon as Roux returns.

In the corner, the Blacksmith stirs.

"Would you like some tea?" Gauge asks.

The Blacksmith pushes himself up and coughs into his sleeve. When he removes his arm, a splattering of blood shines against the linen.

Gauge's breath catches.

(The faint smell of licorice and tobacco tugs me toward the smithy. I begin licking my coat, determined to resist. But I can only put off making an appearance for so long. Eventually he'll set sail, and I'll be compelled to carry out my duty. Hopefully, fortune will grant me a window to retrieve the Blacksmith's soul when Gauge is out of the room.)

"I need you to help me," the Blacksmith rasps.

"Of course," the boy says, wondering what the Blacksmith has in mind.

The Blacksmith reaches under his mattress and pulls out a heart-shaped charm forged of metal. The sides are ragged. "I'd hoped to finish it when Yanis returned, but I fear . . ."

His words trail off as he turns his head to face the wall.

"I don't know much about working metal," the boy says honestly. In truth, he's eager to try—eager for anything that might take his mind off his troubles.

"It's your strength I need," the Blacksmith says.

Gauge helps the man make his way into the shop. The boy's chest tightens. His grandpapá leaned on him in much the same way not so long ago.

The Blacksmith sinks onto a stool in front of a sandstone wheel that hangs vertically in a wooden frame. It's almost identical to the grindstone in the Carpenter's shop, the one they used to sharpen their tools. This one is operated by a crank sticking out from the frame rather than by a foot treadle.

Gauge glances toward the door, half-expecting a Guard to pound on it any moment. Bright sunlight sneaks in around the edges of the shades.

"I'll fetch the water," the boy says.

A small pail with a lip for pouring rests near the grindstone. Gauge fills the pail in the back, taking care not to slosh water on the floor as he passes through the living room.

"Well done," the Blacksmith says, accepting the pail. "Now start cranking."

The grindstone creaks and then begins to spin. The Blacksmith pours a thin stream over the wheel. He hands the pail to Gauge, who stops turning the crank to set the pail down.

The old man pulls the heart from his pocket.

Gauge resumes cranking. The Blacksmith holds the heart up against the stone. A grating sound fills the air.

"That's it," the Blacksmith says. "Smooth and steady."

Gauge's shoulder is already starting to burn from the effort, but he continues cranking. The happiness shining in the Blacksmith's eyes reminds him of his grandpapá, how content he was whittling away at a block of wood or shaping the delicate curve of a cabinet. The old man taught Gauge everything he knew, everything he had learned from *his* father, who was taught by his father before, and so on, as far back as anyone could remember. Gauge's chest tightens as he imagines the tradition ending with him.

"Whoa," the Blacksmith says, "not so fast."

Gauge isn't sure when he sped up. He slows his pace, tries to steady his breath. They work only a few more moments before the Blacksmith motions for Gauge to stop. "That's enough for today."

The edges of the heart are still jagged. "But we can—"

"Another time," the Blacksmith rasps. "Help me back to bed."

Tucked in, the Blacksmith presses the heart into Gauge's palm and squeezes both their fingers around it. "Bastien the Carpenter had a good heart," he says. "I see the same in you. Whatever happens, promise me you'll take care of things."

Gauge senses the Blacksmith is talking about more than the metal heart. His own heart pumps like a treadle working at full speed. Without the Blacksmith, how will he get on the ship?

The old man coughs.

"We can finish tomorrow," Gauge says. "You can give it to her yourself."

"Promise!" the Blacksmith wheezes.

Gauge is unnerved by the Blacksmith's insistence. Surely, he must know Gauge can't risk staying.

Roux bursts in the door waving a piece of paper, her eyes wide with panic. "Your face is everywhere!"

The Blacksmith squeezes Gauge's hand and lets his head sink to his pillow.

The boy slips the heart in his pocket. "What are you talking about?"

She passes him the paper. "They're posted all over the village. There's no mistaking your curls."

Gauge's face stares up at him. It's not a very good likeness—they have his chin pointed where it should be square, and they got his mouth and eyes wrong, too. But Roux is right—the curls give him away.

(In all fairness, the artist was under tremendous pressure to create a portrait based on nothing more than a vague description from the Steward, who was still too traumatized by her brush with the Voyant to provide useful details.)

Gauge sinks down in front of the hearth. How can he possibly hope to go for his knife when every person in the village knows him? "That's it, then. I'm done for."

A coughing attack takes over the Blacksmith. Roux rushes to his side. "Father, is there no improvement?"

Between coughs she adds, "Is there anything I can fetch for you?"

"Leave me to rest," he whispers.

Roux kisses her father's cheek and tucks his blanket up under his chin. Gauge looks away, wishing he could give them some time alone. But where would he go? He might as well have a target marked on his forehead. He buries his head in his arms. The shop has been his entire life. He can't imagine how he'll start over someplace else.

Roux prepares him a cup of tea. The scalding liquid burns Gauge's tongue, numbs his taste buds. He swallows, relishing the pain.

Roux fills a bowl with water and places it next to him.

"What's that for?"

She pulls out a razor. Gauge feels his cheeks, perplexed. He hasn't started shaving yet.

"Bend your head," Roux says.

"What?"

"We have to change your appearance."

The boy raises his hands to his hair. "But I—I'll be bald!"

"Better bald than set out to sea."

He knows she's right, but he's not ready to admit it. "They'll recognize my face."

"Maybe. But we'll blacken your teeth with tea, stain your nails with ashes—maybe even add a streak or two on your face. They'll never expect a Carpenter's Apprentice to look like he runs the forge."

"Shaving me bald will be too obvious. I might as well announce I'm the curly-haired boy they're looking for."

Roux places her hands on her hips. "What do you suggest?"

"Scissors," Gauge says, adjusting to the idea. "You can cut it down nearly to my head."

"For death's sake," Roux says. "Are you always this vain?"

Gauge's cheeks burn. He never thought of himself as vain. But his hair is—he already lost so much of himself, of his previous life. Grandpapá always said how much Gauge's curls reminded the old man of the boy's mother. This is one thing he might be able to hold onto. (I can't blame the boy. After all this time, I continue to wish for the thick tresses I once had.

There's something about having hair that's deeply personal—*human*. If I ever get mine back, I'll never allow anyone to cut it. Never.)

Huffing, Roux puts away the razor and fetches a sharpened pair of scissors from the shop.

Gauge eyes her warily as she approaches. "You know what you're doing with those things?"

"You're welcome to do it yourself if you'd like."

Gauge's eyes water. He never had to do it himself—Grandpapá always cut his hair.

"Watch the ears," he says.

"It's that tongue you need to worry about."

Roux reaches for his head, enveloping him in a cloud of lavender. It's different than his grandpapá's earthy scent but not unpleasant. Before long, a pile of discarded curls litters the floor, a reminder of the life he's leaving behind.

Roux drops the scissors to her side. "Hardly recognize you. Now sit still while I fetch a cool cinder."

Once she's gone, Gauge runs his hand over his head. He never thought of his curls as weighing him down, but he feels lighter. He wonders how he looks, if Roux likes his hair this way, then he blushes. It doesn't matter what she thinks.

Roux returns with a cinder wrapped in a hand-kerchief. "Rub this under your nails. Smear a streak across your cheek and smudge your clothes."

The boy begins scraping at the coal with his nails.

"Over the fire," Roux says sharply. "I have enough to do without cleaning up after you."

The Blacksmith moans.

"Father?" Roux bends over the Blacksmith. His eyes flutter open. He attempts to cough, but it catches in his throat. His breathing is shallow, panicked. He's not ready to go, not ready to leave his daughter.

(These cases are always the hardest. Children aren't afraid of me at all, and the elderly are generally tired, ready to begin their journeys to the Sea-in-the-Sky. But those in the middle fight leaving their dead bodies. As though remaining might somehow gift them another shot at life.)

"Father," Roux says again, "are you all right?"

The Blacksmith doesn't answer.

"He's clammy," Roux says.

The Blacksmith tries again to cough but can't catch his breath.

"I need to go for Nicoline the Healer," Roux says.

"Let me go," Gauge says, remembering how he stayed in bed when his grandpapá was ill.

Their gazes meet. Roux is desperate to stay with her father, but if Gauge is recognized . . .

The Blacksmith wheezes.

"Hurry," she pleads.

The boy rubs his dirty hands across a cheek and then wipes them on his clothes, hoping it's enough. With a last look at Roux and her ailing father, he tosses the cinder on the hearth and rushes for the door. Again the Blacksmith wheezes; there is no time to lose.

(Nobody can outrun death. Trust me—I tried to save my daughter. But the boy will do his best, and I suppose that's all anyone can ask.)

Chapter Seven

Rushing through the streets, the boy doesn't see the muddy patches of ice, the dilapidated signs, the once-proud buildings now worn and sagging as their owners pay ever-increasing taxes to Lord Mayor Vulpine. He sees everything as it was winters before, when he ran errands with his grandpapá, when he played openly in the wind-kissed streets, when shop owners could still care for their properties.

His reverie is broken when he passes the first poster bearing his face. He runs his hand through his shorn hair, hoping it's enough of a change.

He'd rather avoid passing his grandpapá's shop, but it's the most efficient route, and it gives him the chance to see if Guards are posted. Out of the corner of his eye, he spots broken glass all over the cobblestone street. Longing pierces Gauge's stomach, sharper than the glass. He'd give anything to be in the workshop, the comforting feel of wood in his hands, his grandpapá's gentle instructions guiding his way.

A Guard stands at attention by the now-closed door. He notices Gauge. "You there," he yells. "Stop!"

The boy twists around but doesn't slow. "No time," he yells. "I have to fetch a Healer."

He can't believe it when the Guard accepts his explanation.

Gauge snakes through the streets until he arrives at a brick home resting on the square, directly across from Lord Mayor Vulpine's towering abode. This home is much smaller, but tidy and inviting. The blue shutters appear freshly painted. The boy pounds on the door.

"Hello," he calls. "Anyone home?"

Faint footsteps echo inside, becoming louder.

The door swings open, clouding Gauge in the overwhelming scent of what he guesses must be the Healer's many herbs and remedies.

"No need to break my door down," a freckle-skinned lady in strange attire grumbles.

Instead of pantaloons, she wears a gown that looks suspiciously like a gunnysack, the kind used to haul potatoes. And she's wearing an odd pair of shoes that make it appear as though she's on a raised platform. One side of her head is shaved clean while the hair on the other side reaches her shoulders. Piercings line her ears. (How times have changed. In my day, piercings were risky business, prone to infection and hardly worth it.)

"Can I help you?"

"I'm seeking Nicoline the Healer," the boy mumbles, keeping his head down in the hope that he won't be recognized.

"And so you've found her. What of it?"

Gauge can't guess at the woman's age. Older than an Apprentice, too young to be a grandmother. "It's Woolsey the Blacksmith," he says. "You must come quickly."

Her shoulders straighten and she drops her grumpy tone. "Let me fetch my bag."

Gauge chews nervously on a nail. He can't help but

wonder if the Healer could have saved his grandpapá. He shakes his head. His grandpapá always said there's no sense crying over a sunken boat. Right now, he has to focus on saving the Blacksmith.

He peers inside the cracked-open door, expecting to find any number of curiosities. But the home is humble and warm, featuring a simple trestle table (one he doesn't recognize as being his grandpapá's work) and two stools. A fur spread in front of the fireplace adds comfort to the room, as does a woven tapestry on the wall.

The Healer returns, carrying a bag bulging with supplies.

"Lead the way," she says.

Gauge breathes easier on the return, knowing no one will look for the Voyant at the Healer's side.

They arrive back at the smithy, where the Healer immediately takes charge. She asks for a pot of boiling water, which Roux has at the ready. The Healer pulls a bewildering assortment of herbs from her pouch and sorts them on the table.

Gauge fetches another armload of wood and fresh water and then hovers nearby. The Blacksmith hasn't opened his eyes and still struggles for breath. Gauge is torn between wanting to stay, to offer what comfort and help he can, and retrieving his knife.

The Healer trips over his feet on her way to the fire. "Stay out of the way," she snaps.

"Sorry," Gauge says, inching toward the door.

Roux kneels by her father's side, gripping his hand and stroking his forehead.

The boy tells himself it's better if he's not underfoot and slips outside. Shadows stretch long on the ground, signaling that he must hurry if he's to stand any chance of retrieving his knife before nightfall. He doesn't know when—or if—I will make another appearance, but if I do, he plans to be ready. (As close to ready as a boy could be to fight a magical Wolf, anyway.)

He's not surprised to find the Guard still standing in front of the shop. Instead of turning down the street, he stuffs his hands in his pockets, lowers his head, and continues on to the alley, hoping Lord Mayor Vulpine won't have wasted resources posting another Guard at the back door. He reaches Claude the Potter's yard and ducks behind the tall, wall-like fence that begins at the back of the Potter's building and continues to the alley, hiding the Carpenter's shop and backyard from the Potter's view.

Gauge peeks around the edge, ignoring the stack of lumber and the mud-crusted garden, both patiently awaiting his grandpapá's attention, both unaware that the old man is gone. A Guard rests on a log meant for firewood, his attention fixed on the hunk of bread in his hand. (The Guard's attention isn't on the bread at all. He's thinking about the pretty girl he passed on the way over, wondering if she'll accept an invitation to walk along the beach with him.)

Gauge pulls back and presses himself against the wall, breathing heavily. This was a terrible idea. Had he really thought he'd be able to waltz inside and reclaim his knife? Lord Mayor Vulpine will go to any lengths to capture him—including posting Guards at both doors day and night.

The boy sets his jaw. If he's going to be forced to get on a ship in four days, to leave behind everything he knows and loves, he isn't going without taking his knife with him. Besides, he has to have *something* to protect himself from me. From whatever is to come.

He chews on his lip as he formulates a plan. If he can't enter through the front or back doors, he'll have to go through the side window, only accessible from the small aisle between his place and the Potter's. Since there's no way for him to reach the window from the Potter's fenced yard, that means he's going to have to come from the Potter's roof. Crates, presumably to ship his wares, are scattered at the back of the Potter's building.

After waiting to make sure there are no signs of movement inside the Potter's living room, Gauge stacks the crates into a tower as best he can. He scrambles up, using his strength to pull himself onto the roof.

Crouching low and moving slowly, he edges along until he's directly over the window leading into his grandpapá's living room. The ground is farther away than he thought, but he lowers himself over the side and then drops through the air.

He lands harder than expected and tenses, waiting to find out if the Guards will investigate. After several moments, he springs into action, braving a rosebush to raise the window and squirm through, landing on the bed he once shared with his grandpapá.

He thinks he can see the indentation from the old man's body. His breath catches as he remembers all the nights he spent curled up against his grandpapá's warm back and the painful moments after he first discovered the old man had set sail.

He scans the rest of the room. A spider has moved in, spinning a web across the front of the hearth, claiming it for her own. Gauge remembers the time a black widow crawled across the table while he and Grandpapá were eating.

Gauge was terrified of being bitten, but now he'd gladly face the spider if it meant he could hear his grandpapá's voice as he ushered the spider outside, reminding Gauge that every life is worthy of respect.

Gauge flashes to another scene, sees himself as a young boy pushing his toy boat around the floor in front of the fire.

Gauge, the old man calls from the shop, *give me a hand, would you?*

Just a moment, Grandpapá, Gauge calls back.

Heavy footsteps sound from the front, pulling the boy from his imaginings. The footsteps move toward the living room. Gauge lunges for his pillow, feels for his knife, finds nothing.

The footsteps move closer.

Gauge casts a last, desperate glance over the bed and then dives out the window. The rosebush tears at his skin, attempting to slow his exit. The door opens the very moment he hits the ground. He holds his breath, waits as footsteps circle the room. He doesn't know if this is a third Guard or the Guard from the front doing rounds—either way, he realizes how silly it was to come, to risk everything for a knife.

He's tempted to bolt for the front of the building, to make a run for it, but it's too risky. If there is a Guard out front, his chance of escape will be low. And Lord Mayor Vulpine will only redouble his efforts if the boy is spotted in the village.

Gauge realizes he has another problem—a big one.

Without the crates, he has no way to get back on the Potter's roof.

He thinks he smells a wet dog. (He doesn't, but the brain loves nothing better than to play tricks on people when they are most afraid.) He swallows, desperate to put as much distance between himself and this place as possible in case I make an appearance. He scans for an escape. The Potter's window! It's propped open, close enough that the boy can reach it in only a few steps.

He peeks inside and breathes a sigh of relief—the room is empty. The boy pushes the window open and scrambles inside. The living room is nearly identical to the one he shared with his grandpapá except the walls are covered in shelves lined with colorful bowls, plates, and pitchers of all shapes and sizes. Gauge tiptoes through as quickly as he dares, intent on escaping through the back door.

He's only cracked it open when the hair on the back of his neck stands up, warning him he's not alone.

He spins around to find the Potter's young daughter in the doorway from the shop, her thumb in her mouth. (A habit I could never understand, though it certainly brought my daughter plenty of comfort.) She stares at him, her honey-colored eyes wide and curious.

Gauge fumbles in his pocket, searching for something to trade for the girl's silence. He pulls out a single feather, one he must have overlooked, and offers it to the girl. She doesn't move. The boy sets the feather on the floor, slips out the door, and races down the alley, his heart pounding.

After reaching the street, he assures himself that he's not being followed and slows. Despite his escape, he hangs his head, beating himself up for failing to find his knife.

He stumbles through the village, not wanting to return to the smithy but without any idea where else he might find shelter. He ducks into an unfamiliar alley, hoping to buy time while he formulates a plan. A mangy mastiff approaches, its teeth bared. Gauge freezes. How is he to fight an angry dog with his bare hands?

(The dog is more than angry. She recently gave birth and is desperate for food in order to keep her milk flowing. There can be no doubt that the boy is in grave danger.)

The boy edges backward. "Easy, pup. I'm not looking for trouble."

The dog's ears drop back flat against her mud-colored head and she lifts her lip, revealing more razor-sharp teeth.

I'm obviously going to have to intervene. Voyants are too few and far between to let another one die on me. I appear behind Gauge, my hackles raised, my own teeth bared. I make no noise, hoping I can scare off the dog and take my leave before the boy catches wind of my presence.

It almost works. The dog, who is much more in tune with the universe than any human could ever hope to be, has no trouble seeing me. She whimpers and lowers her tail between her legs. With a final, longing glance at Gauge, she turns and slinks away.

Gauge is both stunned and bewildered by the mastiff's sudden change of heart. He sniffs, catches a whiff of something harsher, something wilder than the dog he just faced.

He whirls around.

His eyes widen. He's sure I saved him from the dog only to claim him for myself. He drops into a crouch and tenses, prepared to fight.

The boy's eyes shine with exhaustion.

This is it—my chance to get him to listen. "I'm not going to hurt you."

"Then go away," he says. "Leave me alone."

I step back, hoping he'll relax. "I only want to talk. To help you."

"I don't want your help," the boy cries. "Why do you keep following me—why won't you leave me alone?"

"I want to offer you a job."

"A job?" The boy squeezes his fists tighter. "Have you lost your feathers? There's no way I'd work with you, not for all the shells on the shore." He looks at me as though I'm a pile of rotting whale guts and turns to run away.

I appear in front of him, blocking his path.

Gauge's mouth drops open. He's used to me coming and going, but he has never seen me disappear, much less reappear in a different spot. (I'm not sure *how* I do this; I just do. I suppose it's a bit like dropping a handful of salt into warm water: one second it's there, and then it dissolves. Only I show up somewhere else the very next instant.)

The boy's eyes are wide. He backs away from me.

A memory flashes in my mind, one I haven't thought of in centuries. I was a young girl, no more than ten winters, fetching water from the well. On the way home, I had the sensation that I was being watched. I looked up to find a lynx perched on a branch overhead. I froze, so filled with terror that I couldn't react, couldn't move a muscle. Eventually I regained my senses and backed slowly away before turning around and breaking into a run.

Looking into Gauge's eyes now, I see the same fear, the same desire to escape.

I hang my head, defeated. "The world isn't what you think," I say. "*I'm* not what you think."

"I don't care what you are," the boy snarls.

I tuck my tail between my legs and disappear. A moment later, I'm hurtling through the countryside, chasing a fallow deer that zigs and zags every which way. I don't want to catch it, only need some release for the frustration that brews inside of me. Why won't the boy see that I'm trying to help him?

Gauge nearly breaks into a run, but he doesn't dare draw attention to himself. He walks quickly along the streets, his gaze darting side to side as he strains to see with what's left of the quickly fading light. He can't understand why I followed him, why I saved him. He can't believe that I actually want to offer him a job. *It must be a trick.*

He imagines that I'm waiting for him to let down his guard, that as soon as he does, I'll make my move. He can't lead me back to the smithy.

The boy drifts through the streets like a ship lost at sea. Longing surges through him, a desperation to see his grandpapá. He's sure that if only the old man were here, he'd know exactly what to do. Without meaning to, the boy eventually finds himself near the Wharves. He thinks about his grandpapá's body, left to the weather and vultures.

Two Guards are posted, men easily twice his size, one with skin the color of birch and a slightly older one with skin closer to ebony, both wearing yellow sashes.

"What do you want?" the older man asks.

"Here to bury the Carpenter." The words slip out, a surprise even to Gauge. But now that he's said them, he wants to do it. Needs to do it. Out of respect and because his muscles are tense, aching for release.

"By whose orders?"

"Lord Mayor Vulpine."

"All alone?"

"I'm the only one who will do it," Gauge says, raising his chin. "The others are too scared."

"Can't hardly blame them," the younger Guard says.

He's smaller, twitchier. Like an ugly rat. Gauge dislikes him immediately. (I can hardly blame him—the man is exactly the sort I would have once crossed the street to avoid.)

The twitchy Guard continues, "Wouldn't want nothing to do with the relation of a Voyant if it was me."

The boy fights to keep the anger from his face. "I'm not scared of a stinking Voyant."

"It's too dark," the older Guard says.

Gauge detects a note of kindness in his voice.

"Come back tomorrow."

"You think I've nothing to do but hang around burying old men? Tomorrow I'll be working. Anyway, Lord Mayor Vulpine ordered it done tonight."

"Let him in," the twitchy Guard says, shrugging. "It's his skin."

The Guards step aside.

"You'll find ropes and shovels in the lean-to," the

older Guard says. Gauge has no idea what possessed him to come here, to put himself in such danger, but he's past caring.

His feeling of defiance lasts until he approaches his grandpapá's grave, rope and shovel in hand. The weather and birds haven't yet begun to work on the body. For a moment, it appears as if the old man might open his eyes, might sit up and go about his day. Gauge's breath catches in his chest. He drops the ropes and shovel, reminding himself that this isn't his grandpapá—only an empty shell.

He notices the broken mirror left behind in the Steward's rush to escape. He snatches the two halves and tucks them in his pocket. It's not his knife, but the weight offers some comfort.

The boy raises his face to the sky, but a thick blanket of clouds block all the lanterns save a patch far off on the horizon, providing the dimmest of light.

He has to get to work.

If he's lucky, if he moves fast enough, he might be able to lower the vessel without dumping his grandpapá's body. Gauge slips a rope through three rings along the top of one side of the vessel—one ring on the left, one in the middle, and one on the right—and then knots the ends of the rope together, forming a loop.

Another rope would normally be looped on the other side of the vessel and used to lower it carefully into the hole (a task requiring at least two people, preferably more). But with Gauge working alone, the old man is in for a bit of a bumpy ride. The boy positions the vessel so it's perched on the edge of the hole.

He stretches the loop across the hole as he walks around it and then rests the rope over his shoulder, facing away from the hole. If he lunges forward and then releases the rope, the vessel should scoot directly over the hole and then plunge to the bottom.

(This might be the worst idea anyone ever had, but the kid deserves credit for his ingenuity. Not to mention his determination.)

Gauge takes a deep breath, figures how hard he has to pull.

"You forgot your scarf."

The older Guard's voice startles Gauge. He drops the rope and spins around.

The vessel teeters and then settles. The Guard has taken off his sash and tied it around his head to cover his mouth. Instead of accusations or fear, his eyes hold only curiosity.

"Oh, um, yes," Gauge stutters. It's the last thing on his mind, but he doesn't want to arouse any more suspicion. He pulls the wrinkled scarf from the Steward out of his pocket and ties it over his mouth.

The Guard nods, satisfied. Then he motions toward the vessel. "By the looks of it, you could use a hand."

Gauge doesn't know why the Guard is offering to help and is wary of trusting the seemingly kind man's intentions.

"I've got this," Gauge says.

"Could have fooled me. The old man is more likely to end up face-first in the dirt than in the vessel."

"What would you have me do?" the boy asks. He tucks his chin, wishing he still had his curls to hide behind. "Leave the job unfinished?"

The Guard picks up another rope. He slides it through the three rings on his side of the vessel and then ties the ends together.

"Between the two of us, we should be able to get it done."

"You're going to help me?"

"I had a son once," the Guard says. "Would have been about your age." (Though the Healer told the man his son died of a tooth-worm infestation, there isn't any such thing. The boy died of an infection, plain and simple.)

Gauge digs at the ground with his toe.

"Anyway, I don't have anything better to do." The older Guard nods at the younger Guard, who is glowering from his spot at the gate. "That knucklehead never stops yammering. Makes for a long shift. Now let's get this over with."

He wraps the rope tightly around his hand.

Gauge gathers the rope and begins tugging. The vessel wobbles and then begins scooting toward Gauge. It's heavier than he imagined. He grunts and clenches his jaw but holds the rope steady as they begin lowering the vessel in the hole.

Gauge's palms burn as the rope slides through them. Once, he loses his grip, but he manages to find it again before any harm is done. Finally, the vessel lands with a muffled thump.

"Thank you," Gauge says, fighting to keep the tremor from his voice.

"It's no problem," the Guard says. "But you're on your own from here on out. And I'd suggest you get a move on it. My partner over there has taken it to mind that you look like the pictures of the Voyant posted all over the village."

Gauge gulps. "The Voyant would have to be awfully stupid to risk coming here."

The Guard raises his eyebrows. "That he would," he says. "Like I said, I'd finish up if I were you."

Without another word, he returns to the front gate, whistling a cheerful tune.

Gauge's heart pounds out a warning. *The Guard knows. The Guard knows. The Guard knows.*

He eyes the staircase he and Roux used the previous day, thinking that maybe he should make a run for it. But now that he's decided to bury his grandpapá, he won't give up.

The boy sinks his shovel into the mound of thick, heavy soil. He thrusts his boot on top of the blade to push it in. His muscles strain as he lifts out a load and drops it into the hole, where it plops onto his grand-papá's chest.

"May you reach the Sea-in-the-Sky and sail into eternity," he says.

He scoops another shovelful of dirt, taking his grief out on the pile in front of him.

The rat-Guard's gaze burns into his back.

Chapter Eight

It takes Gauge the better part of an hour to fill the hole. With each scoop of dirt, the shovel grows heavier.

Releasing his grandpapá was one thing; burying his body is quite another. There is no escaping the fact that the old man is truly gone. That whatever happens next, the boy is on his own.

He wants to linger by the grave, finds comfort in the waves lapping and gulls squawking. He knows the old man has departed for the Sea-in-the-Sky but longs to tell his grandpapá about all that transpired, believes the old man is listening. With the Guard's eyes taking in his every move, he doesn't dare.

He pats down the dirt, wishing he had a compass to leave on the grave. But the old man always claimed he was an expert at navigating by the lanterns in the sky—he'll find the way. The boy returns the ropes and shovel to the lean-to and exits the Wharves.

The small, twitchy Guard grabs his elbow, spinning him around. "Your face—I'm sure I've seen it somewhere."

Without Roux there to save him, Gauge has to think fast. "You've probably seen me around. I'm a back-up. I help carry the vessels when one of the regular crew gets sick."

The Guard peers at him. "Hmmm," he says. "Don't suppose you've had a haircut recently?"

"Every Sunday," Gauge says, running his hand over his clipped head. "The Blacksmith says long hair is dangerous near the fire."

"Let him go," the older Guard says, feigning boredom. "Look at him—he's obviously not the Carpenter's boy."

"I don't know," the twitchy Guard says. "There's something about his eyes that reminds me of the posters."

"Now you're letting your imagination run wild," the older Guard says.

"Nothing wrong with that, not if it earns me a nice bag of shells."

"Stop being a mud sucker," the older Guard says.

He jerks his head and addresses Gauge. "Go on, get out of here."

His heart pounding louder than his grandpapá's hammer, Gauge slips away, forcing himself not to run. He's going to have to be a lot more careful from now on. He's been lucky so far, but his grandpapá always used to say that the problem with luck is that it always runs out eventually.

The thought reminds the boy of the run-in he had with the stray dog, how I appeared and then disappeared. The broken mirror weighs down one pocket. His hand slips into the other and finds the cold metal heart.

He doesn't want to return to the smithy, but he has nowhere else to go. He turns the heart in his hand, reminding himself that he has to return it. Besides, he needs the Blacksmith's help boarding the ship.

Gauge arrives back at the smithy expecting to find the Blacksmith resting comfortably, but Roux remains beside her father, her face buried in his chest.

The Healer rocks in the Blacksmith's chair. She gives a single shake of her head, indicating the news isn't good.

Gauge plops down on the hearth. The Blacksmith's chest heaves as he gasps for air. His head has been shaved bald.

"What happened to his hair?" Gauge asks. He's not sure why the sight makes him uncomfortable— it's not as if the Blacksmith had much hair anyway. But somehow, seeing his naked head feels to Gauge as though he caught the man without any clothes.

"It's . . . to help prepare him for his journey."

(The less he weighs, they believe, the easier it will be to reach the Sea-in-the-Sky. By now I hope you know better than to ask how the weight of the body affects the soul reaching the sky.)

Roux lets out a wretched sob.

Gauge ponders the Healer's words. Why didn't the Steward do the same for his grandpapá?

"If my—" He stops himself. "If someone sets sail with all their hair, will they still reach the Sea-in-the-Sky?"

"They don't have to worry," the Healer says. "We

don't always have the opportunity to shave before someone sets sail."

"Can't you do it after?"

"I suppose you could—but most people don't care to spend so much time that close to the body."

"It really doesn't matter?"

"I wouldn't say that," the Healer says thoughtfully. "Only that it's more tradition than it is necessity."

Gauge doesn't understand the difference, but the Healer's reassuring words lift the heavy rock pressing on his chest.

The hair Roux cut from Gauge's head earlier dirties the floor. He attempts to gather it under his feet, hoping the Healer hasn't noticed.

The Blacksmith wheezes.

"What's wrong with him?" Gauge asks. "Is it the wasting disease?"

"Gets 'em all, eventually," the Healer says.

"How come?"

"Breathing in the smoke all day isn't good for their lungs. Chars 'em from the inside out."

Gauge's chest tightens again as he imagines his lungs blackening, refusing to pull in air.

"Rest easy," the Healer says. "I suspect you'll be spared."

The boy shifts, wondering if she knows he's not the Blacksmith's Apprentice.

Roux's shoulders heave. She raises her head, revealing a tear-stained face. "Will it hurt terribly?"

"Children lose their teeth before new ones grow. Leaves fall off the trees in fall and return in the spring. The sun sets at night but rises every morning."

"Are you saying you don't know?" Roux asks.

"I'm saying it isn't easy to accept what we can't understand. But one thing I know to be true is that light always follows the dark."

The pain in Gauge's chest is fiery and raw. But maybe his grandpapá is in a better place now. Soon, the Blacksmith will be, too.

Roux strokes the Blacksmith's hand. "Go ahead, Father. I know you're hanging on for me. But I'll be fine. Go. You'll feel better once you reach the Sea-in-the-Sky."

Fresh tears leak from her eyes. Gauge admires her bravery.

He loved his grandpapá more than anybody in the

world. If he had known death was coming, he would have begged the old man to fight it, to stay at all costs. But that would have been selfish. Watching Roux, he can't help but think that sometimes the best way to love somebody might be to let them set sail.

The night passes slowly. The boy would give anything to sleep, but he doesn't dare. Although he doesn't know if I've tracked him to the smithy, my appearance on the street was enough to convince him that I could appear anytime, anywhere. The boy's fingers itch to work, to channel his emotions into something productive. Grandpapá always said there was no finer pastime than carving, that it was an act of creation. Of rejuvenation. He taught Gauge to search for the beauty locked inside a piece of wood, to judge it based not on what it was but on what it might become.

Gauge watches the fire crackle and pop as it eats away at the blazing logs.

The moment the Healer dozes in the rocking chair, the boy scoops the hair from under his feet and throws it in the fire. His sigh of relief turns to revulsion as the foul smell of burning hair poisons the air. Gauge pinches his nose and breathes through his mouth, hoping the odor doesn't call the attention of the Healer.

She shifts but doesn't wake. Roux doesn't so much as move from her father's side. Gauge finally gives in to his exhaustion and settles at the table, where he lets his head sink into his arms. His dreams are wild and frightening fragments—Grandpapá's vessel teetering in the sky. Gauge in a boat with one oar, paddling furiously but only spinning in circles as sharks close in. The Wolf, tugging at Gauge's feet while he watches, unable to move.

It's early morning when he awakes to a sharp cry.

"Help!" Roux yells.

The boy's hand immediately reaches for the knife that's not there.

The Blacksmith takes a series of deep, rattling breaths.

The Healer joins Roux at the Blacksmith's side. "It won't be long now," she says, resting a hand on the girl's shoulder.

"No!" Roux cries. "Please, help him!"

The Blacksmith's breathing pauses. The boy wonders if the end has come. The Blacksmith takes another breath, releases it. Gauge waits for him to suck in again. He never does.

(Don't look at me like that. I never promised you a picnic on the beach.)

Roux throws herself across her father's body. "No, Father, don't go. I know I said you could, but I take it back. I didn't mean it. I need you. Don't leave me, Father, please."

Gauge's own loss rises up, forming a lump in his throat. He thinks of all the things he wishes he could have said to his grandpapá—how he would have thanked the old man for always being there, for saving him from Lord Mayor Vulpine. For loving him.

The Healer ties a white scarf around her mouth, hands scarves to Roux and Gauge, and then closes the Blacksmith's vacant eyes. "May you sail in peace."

"May you sail in peace," Gauge mumbles into the scarf. He feels as though he should say some kind of goodbye to the Blacksmith, thank him for offering shelter and safety. Gauge fumbles for the heart in his pocket and grips the cool metal in his warm hand. "I'll finish it for you," he whispers. "I promise."

The Healer begins packing her supplies.

"That's it—you're going to leave?" Gauge asks.

"There's nothing more to be done," the Healer says. "I'll send word to Mistress Charbonneaux. She'll arrange for the Release."

The boy's nails dig into his palms. The Release. The Steward.

Roux makes no move to acknowledge the Healer.

"Thank you," Gauge says for her.

The Healer clears her throat. "There's the matter of payment."

"Payment for what—you didn't save him!" Gauge says.

"I don't choose who sets sail," she says gently. "But my time is worth twenty shells."

Her gaze flickers toward Roux. "The two of you are going to be in for a rough go of it on your own. I'll open an account, accept one shell every fortnight."

She pauses at the door. "There is one more thing."

"What's that?" Gauge asks.

The Healer hesitates. "The questions you asked earlier . . ."

"Yes," Gauge says, not sure exactly what she's referring to but desperate for her to share something, anything, to help him continue on through his pain, to help Roux face hers.

Roux groans, drawing the Healer's attention.

The Healer sags like a punctured water bladder and shakes her head.

"Now isn't the time. But when you find the answers you seek, remember this: the Steward—she's only doing her job."

She disappears out the door, leaving Gauge to stare after her. He doesn't know what the Steward has to do with anything. He decides the Healer must be one fish short of a haul and tucks away his frustration.

Roux is still bent over her father's body.

Gauge places his hand on Roux's shoulder. "The Steward will be here soon."

Roux doesn't lift her head.

"I'm sorry to leave you, but I should go."

She doesn't move.

"Roux, did you hear me?"

"Don't go," she whispers. She lifts her face. Her eyes are unfocused, shocked.

"I have to," Gauge says, wishing for all the world it wasn't true.

"Hide," Roux pleads.

Gauge's instincts tell him to run, to get as far from the Steward as possible. "I can't let her see me. It's unsafe—for both of us."

Roux jumps to her feet, filled with a sudden, frenetic energy. "I'd better get the water on in case she wants a cup of tea."

The boy remembers the Steward's efficiency when she came for his grandpapá. He's certain she won't want tea, but—sensing Roux's need to stay busy—he doesn't say anything and instead lingers by the back door while she rushes about the small room. He can't abandon her, not now.

A knock sounds at the front door as the pot of water comes to a boil.

"Quick," Roux says. "In the forge!"

The boy remembers his leg cramp and the spider crawling in his ear. "I'll wait out back."

He lets himself out. Huddled up against the wall, he slips the scarf from his face and gulps fresh air. The wind is brisk, but he comforts himself with the thought that it won't take long to load the Blacksmith's body.

He's starting to shiver when he smells something familiar wafting from inside. He lifts his nose, sniffing deeply. Then he jumps up and peers in the window.

The crew is maneuvering an elaborate vessel through the door from the shop. It's made of cedar and the sides are carved with dolphins frolicking in gentle waves. Gauge frowns. Cedar will stand up well to moisture, but won't its weight prevent the Blacksmith from getting off the ground?

The boy's gaze races to the Blacksmith's body. He catches me nipping at the Blacksmith's feet.

I cringe but continue my work. (If I'd come and gone even moments earlier, I wouldn't have been caught. But I was busy with another soul. I have an entire country to cover, you know. Even though that usually amounts to only two or three souls an hour, it's not like I can control the timing.)

The Blacksmith is angry that his life has been cut short. He's determined to remain exactly where he is. I plant my paws and clench my jaw. Using all my strength, I tug his soul from his feet and let it dangle between my teeth. He squirms and writhes in a desperate attempt to break free.

Gauge's eyes are wide, horrified. At first, he can hardly believe what he's seeing. Then his dream comes rushing back. Anger pulses inside him like a living, breathing thing. He was wrong about me. So wrong. He tells himself that I don't just kill people—I steal their souls. Without taking the time to think what it will mean for himself, he tenses his muscles and prepares to lunge for the door.

Before he can move, I cast what I hope he'll register as an apologetic glance in his direction and hurry out the front.

The crew—oblivious to what happened —sets the vessel next to the bed and begins loading the Blacksmith's body. They'll transport it to the Wharves, where it will await the Release.

The boy clenches both fists and raises them to his head. He's filled with rage, with guilt. How will he tell Roux?

He drops his hands. His chest heaves as he sucks in angry puffs of air and counts the souls he thinks I've stolen. His grandpapá's, Mistress Vulpine's, the Blacksmith's. He's sure there must be more.

A whirl of whistles and chirps fills the air as a

small flock of pigeons rises overhead, circling over the smithy. A minute later, the Steward's piercing whistle sounds and the birds disappear.

The crew carries the vessel—loaded with the Blacksmith's body—into the shop and out the front door.

Gauge waits until he's sure they're gone and then stumbles inside and sinks down on the floor. Roux enters from the shop and pulls off her scarf as she sinks down next to him. He knows he has to tell her. He squirms, blaming himself. If he hadn't come here, if he hadn't stayed, he might have spared her this pain.

A knock sounds at the front door. Gauge jumps up. "I have to go."

"Please," Roux whispers, silently begging him not to leave.

The knock sounds again. Gauge guesses it's the neighbors coming to pay their respects. "They'll know I'm not your father's—I'm not your Apprentice."

"We'll tell them you're new. Please."

Tears shimmer in her eyes.

Reluctantly, Gauge answers the door. He squints into the bright sun.

"I saw the pigeons," a hunched old lady carrying a basket filled with fishing lures announces. "Came to pay my respects. Didn't know the Blacksmith very well, but his wife was a good sort." She stares at Gauge, her watery gray eyes expectant.

"Would you . . . like to come in?" Gauge asks, opening the door wider.

"A cup of tea will be just the thing. Take these lures, won't you?"

She hands Gauge the basket and enters. "There's a dear."

As the boy shuts the door, he notices a fishing net has been strung across its front—to mark the house for those seeking to pay their respects. His lips pinch as he thinks of all the things the Steward should have done—failed to do—for his grandpapá. Not that it matters, not now that he knows the truth. He grits his teeth, struggles to contain his anger.

Before he can close the door, a neighbor emerges from a shop up the street. It's a younger woman with three children tugging at her apron. She carries a loaf of bread and what looks like another loaf wrapped for travel.

"You must be a new Apprentice?" she asks, handing the loaves to Gauge. The smell fills his nose, makes his stomach growl.

"Huh?" he asks.

She raises an eyebrow.

"Oh, yes, the Apprentice. That's me. Please, do come in."

Her children stick close to her side as they cross into the back. (One of them has wispy hair and a pert nose, just like my—never mind. We don't need to talk about that now. Please, do stay focused on the task at hand.)

The next visitor is an older man who walks with a cane, dragging one leg behind him.

"Who are you?" he asks Gauge, peering at him from under a floppy fishing hat.

"Uh, I'm the Apprentice," Gauge says.

"What happened to Yanis?" the old man growls.

Roux appears at Gauge's side. "He was called back to help his parents on the farm. We had to scramble to find a replacement. This is Eli. He's from Montpeyroux."

The old man grunts and brushes by Gauge,

offering Roux a sturdy fishing net. "My son grew up fishing with your father. He was as good as they come," he says. "Hate to see him set sail, but I guess it's a voyage we all have to make eventually."

Roux blinks back tears. "Please, do come in."

The living room is soon packed with neighbors milling about, exchanging news and gossip, complaining about aching joints and Lord Mayor Vulpine's ever-increasing taxes. A stack of gifts they brought to help the Blacksmith set sail towers by the door. A potpourri of sounds and smells fill the room, making Gauge's head swim. He avoids conversation when he can and introduces himself as the new Apprentice when he can't. He's busy slicing a wheel of cheese when a nearby conversation stops him.

"Knowing a Voyant is on the loose has me out of sorts," someone says.

Gauge recognizes the voice as belonging to the woman with all the children. He doesn't dare turn around, but he cocks his head, straining to hear.

"Do you think he's in the village?" another voice asks.

The woman with the children answers. "No

telling. I won't let these three out of my sight until he's found."

"Pray it's before anyone else sets sail."

"Poor Woolsey—he didn't deserve to go like this."

The boy drops the knife, then snatches it back up. They think *he* called death to the Blacksmith? The thought probably shouldn't surprise him, but it does. Even after all he's endured, he can't believe they actually think he's running around the village causing anyone to set sail.

He hunches lower, suddenly aware of how many people surround him. How many people might recognize him. Desperate to blend in, he resumes cutting the cheese.

The knife slips and nicks his finger. "Ouch!"

He puts his finger in his mouth and uses his tongue to stop the blood. The room is uncomfortably warm. He thinks back to the day his grandpapá died. How alone he felt. What would that first day have been like if people had come by to offer him comfort? If he hadn't spent it fearing for his life, for his safety?

He remembers the moment I stole the Blacksmith's soul. Gauge still can't quite believe that what he saw was real. That his dream wasn't a dream at all. There's only one thing left to do. He vows to hunt me down. Make me pay for what he thinks I've done to Roux and her father. To his grandpapá. To *him*.

Gauge tries to hide his shaking hands, but rage and determination fuel his every movement. He forces himself to play his role until late afternoon, when the last guest finally departs.

Roux's face is drawn and tired, but she busies herself wrapping up the leftover cheese, stringing the smoked fish from the rafters, and sorting through the gifts left for the Blacksmith. She straightens. "I've got to get this loaded into the cart."

Her voice is brisk, determined. She won't let herself fall apart—not yet.

"I'll help." Gauge lifts an armload of gifts and deposits them on the delivery cart tucked in the front of the shop, dreading what's to come.

He has to tell her. It doesn't make any sense to go through the trouble of loading the fishing poles, worms, nets, and food into the cart, hauling it all to the Wharves, and attending the Release when the Blacksmith's soul has already been taken. But the words stick in the boy's throat.

Once he tells her, there's no taking it back. He hates himself for it, but he steps aside, watches her push open the massive front doors and wheel the cart outside.

"I'll be back soon," she says.

The boy's grandpapá said the exact same thing the first time he left Gauge alone. While the old man was gone, the boy played with his toy boat, pretending he was exploring the Seven Seas. He expected his grandpapá home in time to prepare dinner. When darkness fell and the old man still hadn't returned, Gauge crawled into bed, too scared to attempt lighting a fire on his own. He pulled the covers up over his head and counted the seconds ticking by.

When his grandpapá finally hobbled home, slowed by a sprained ankle, Gauge threw himself into the old man's arms.

"What's all this?" his grandpapá said. "Why didn't you start a fire?"

Gauge was too embarrassed to admit that he was scared.

Now the boy closes the door behind Roux, longing

to crawl into bed and pull the covers up over his head. But that won't do. His fingers twitch, restless and eager to find some comfort in being busy. Roux's cooking knife will work if I make a sudden return, but it's no good for carving.

Besides, he made the Blacksmith a promise. The boy fetches water and sets himself in front of the grindstone. After wetting it, he turns the crank with one hand, polishing the metal heart with the other. It begins to take on a soft sheen and Gauge blinks back tears. He doesn't know what his own heart looks like, but it must be filled with dents and dings and boast a giant gash right down the middle. It can't be fixed with a grindstone. Maybe it can't be fixed at all.

Chapter Nine

There's no sense in sitting around watching Gauge mope. Let's go along with Roux as she makes her way to the Wharves. Despite her wiry frame, she's used to fetching and delivering heavy items for the Blacksmith and hardly breaks a sweat as she pushes the cart through the village.

She makes good time and the Guards stand aside to let her enter. Arriving at the Blacksmith's vessel, Roux ties her scarf over her mouth, drops to her knees, and reaches for his cold hand. (She has a one-sided conversation with him, too, but we can skip over that. It's all the usual—why-did-you-leave-me-and-what-will-I-do-without-you sort of stuff.)

She doesn't look up again until she hears footsteps.

The veiled Steward sets her bag down next to the vessel. She's still shaken from her previous visit to the Wharves and works quickly, assisting Roux in transferring the supplies from Roux's cart to the open spaces along the Blacksmith's sides and then moving through the Release ceremony (the details of which I won't bother you with since you've been through it once before). After she finishes tucking feathers in around the vessel, a shadow falls across her face. "Where's the lantern?"

Roux tilts her head. "What lantern?"

The Steward sighs. She gave the girl explicit instructions this very morning. The girl indicated she understood, but she must have been in shock. It's all too common, even when the death is expected.

Roux thinks back to the morning, tries to piece together what bits of the conversation she can recall. There was something about a lantern. Her hand flies to her mouth. "I'll run back to the shop and fetch one."

"That's not necessary," the Steward says.

Roux glances up at the sky, which has begun fading from a bright blue to a dull gray. The first lanterns haven't yet been lit. "How will he find his way?"

"He'll manage," the Steward says, flipping closed the flap on her bag. "There will be plenty of other lanterns already in the sky to guide him."

Roux blinks back hot tears. She had one task. One simple task. And she messed it up. "I'm sorry, Father," she whispers.

The Steward rests a hand on Roux's shoulder. "Your father would be proud of how you're holding up. Don't let this trouble you."

Roux clings to the Steward's comforting words, hoping that she's right.

The Steward gives Roux a few moments to say her final goodbyes and then motions for the crew to approach. As they close in, Roux steps back. She watches, numb and disbelieving, as they lower the vessel containing her father's body into the pit.

The Steward invites Roux to scoop a handful of dirt and sprinkle it over the hole. Roux does it, not because she wants to, but because she has to. Because it's what's expected of her. The dirt is wet and clumped from the spring thaw and leaves Roux's hand coated in mud.

She wipes her hand on her skirt and whispers, "Smooth sailing, Father."

. . .

Roux finds herself at the door to the smithy, though she doesn't recall leaving the Wharves, doesn't recall thanking the Steward or moving through the village. She hesitates before opening the door, preparing to walk into the space that always used to be filled with her father's comforting presence.

She draws a deep breath and steps inside. It's worse than she imagined. The Blacksmith's tools sit waiting for his return. She wants to kick the forge and throw his tongs, do something—anything—to make the shop understand that her father is gone, that he's never coming back. Instead, she tucks her head and crosses the smithy.

As she enters the living room, Gauge rises from the rocking chair, feeling the weight of the mostly finished heart in his pocket. (He didn't dare work too long for fear she might return and catch him.)

He knows better than to ask how she's doing and instead sets about making tea. After she has a steaming cup in her hands, Roux speaks, her tearful voice full of self-loathing. "I forgot the lantern."

"What lantern?"

"I was supposed to bring one. To light his way."

The Steward didn't mention any such thing to Gauge during his grandpapá's Release. He pushes aside the thought, not ready to dive into what it means. "Take it now."

"She said he would make his way without it. That there would be plenty of others." She looks up, her eyes filled with anguish. "Do you think she's right? What if he's lost forever in the dark?"

Her pain and guilt distract Gauge. He speaks without thinking. "I'm not sure it matters."

"How dare you!" Roux snaps.

"No!" Gauge says, realizing his mistake. "I didn't mean it like that. Of course your father matters."

She waits for him to explain.

Gauge swallows. He has no choice but to tell the truth. "It's only that—remember when I told you about my dream?"

"Yes, so?"

"Well, um, the Wolf came again. This time, I wasn't sleeping."

For a second, Roux's face is blank. And then she straightens, her eyes sharp. "Came here?"

Gauge nods.

"Are you saying the Wolf . . . ?"

"I think she stole your father's soul."

(Wolves can't roll their eyes. But if we could, mine would be all the way back in my head.)

"When?" Roux's voice is sharp.

"Right before the crew took him away."

"You didn't stop her?"

"The crew was here . . . I didn't know how."

"You sat there and watched it happen?" Her voice rises. "Why didn't you tell me? Why did you let me pack everything up? Why did you let me go to the Release?"

Gauge bows his head. "It happened so quickly. I know I should have told you right away. I couldn't figure out how. I'm sorry."

Roux's hand flies to her mouth and her eyes open wide with horror.

"What?" Gauge asks.

"I overheard one of the women talking today. She said that the Wolf—"

Her voice cracks.

"The Wolf what?" Gauges asks, certain he doesn't

want to know but needing to hear anyway.

"She said the Wolf steals souls to feed to its young down in the Bog."

Revulsion rises in Gauge's throat, thick and bitter. That means his grandpapá didn't make it to the Sea-in-the-Sky—he never stood a chance. And now the Wolf stole the Blacksmith, too. "I'm going to find the Wolf," the boy says. "I won't let it get away with this—I promise."

Roux lifts her gaze to meet his. "You expect me to believe that you are going to track down a magical Wolf and kill it? With what, your bare hands?"

Gauge needs her to believe him. "I'm going to figure it out," he says. "You'll see."

The enormity of what he's committed to crashes down on him. Roux is right—he's set an impossible task for himself. But he's determined. The boy tells himself that *I may be magic, but I'm real. When I appear, I smell like a regular wolf. Look like a regular wolf. Maybe that means he can kill me like a regular wolf.* One way or another, he'll figure out how.

Roux doesn't respond. Gauge senses she needs

time to think, to process. He busies himself preparing a small dinner of leftover bread and cheese, along with a few strips of smoked salmon. They eat in silence. The bread is dry, the salmon tainted with grief. Roux doesn't bother washing her face before peeling off her apron and falling onto her mattress. Gauge starts to pull out the bedding he used the night before. Roux's voice breaks the silence. "No sense in you sleeping on the floor."

Her voice wobbles. Gauge considers arguing, feels as though he's somehow disrespecting the Blacksmith by taking over his sleeping space so soon after he set sail. But she's right.

Gauge slides under the covers. The Blacksmith's scent lingers, reminding the boy of the nights spent before the fire with his grandpapá, lulling him with its promise of security, comfort, and protection. He falls asleep wondering how something that doesn't exist can smell so good.

I've never had a violent streak, but I'll admit that right now I have a tremendous urge to wallop Gauge. All this suffering, all this misery, could be avoided if only he'd listen to my offer. I've never been particularly patient, and it's taking everything I have to allow the boy to continue on with this nonsense about finding me and making me pay.

The boy wakes early, thoughts scurrying about his head like crabs on the beach. All night, he dreamed of the moment he peeked through the window and saw me with the Blacksmith's soul.

He thinks about the Steward assuring Roux that her father didn't need a lantern. The Healer's insistence that having a shaved head wasn't important to the Release. Again, he pictures the Blacksmith's vessel, the heavy cedar and the dolphins carved on the sides. What a contrast to the simple vessel the Steward brought for his grandpapá.

Gauge sits up. The vessel wasn't the only difference. Oars poked out from the Blacksmith's vessel. His grandpapá didn't have any oars at all.

Gauge climbs from bed and paces the room, impervious to the cold air nipping at his cheeks. Lanterns, shaving, oars—if all these things are part of a Release, how come they are so easily dismissed? (My breath catches as I weigh whether or not to make an appearance, to offer the boy the answers he seeks.)

Fearing he might drown in the questions plaguing him, he shakes his head. It hardly matters—not when his grandpapá's and the Blacksmith's souls were stolen. (I let out my breath in a frustrated sigh—I'm the last one Gauge wants to see right now. But at least he's starting to ask questions.)

Roux stirs. The boy isn't sure if she is truly asleep or if she's hiding so she doesn't have to face the world. He can't blame her—if he didn't have me to find, he'd have a hard time getting out of bed, too. He brings in a load of wood, breaks the ice on the water, and fills both the cooking pot and the washing bowl before starting a fire.

He's splashing tepid water on his face when Roux wakes.

"Morning, Father," she mumbles.

The boy freezes. Clears his throat.

Roux's eyes pop open. She sucks in a deep breath and forces herself to begin the day.

Minutes later, she slumps at the table, her grief wrapped around her like a fishing line, threatening to choke her. (Her grief smells of a creamy broth tainted by dead fish, something like clam chowder.)

Gauge doesn't press her for conversation, focuses instead on adding meal to the water once it comes to a boil. He knows grief is most difficult in the morning, when there's no curling back under the covers, no escape from the reality that attacks like a hungry shark. When the gruel is ready, he fills two bowls and sets one in front of Roux.

She pushes her spoon around her bowl but doesn't eat.

Gauge shovels in a bite. A thick lump sticks in his throat. He pushes his bowl back. "What are your plans for today?"

"I need to fetch a chicken."

The boy raises an eyebrow. Grief must have muddled her senses. "What for?"

"If we're going to catch the Wolf, we need something to lure it with. Besides, I'm supposed to put one out anyway. I should have done it last night."

"Why were you supposed to put out a chicken?"

Roux can't believe how little the boy knows of Gatineau's traditions. "If the smell of death tempts the Wolf, it will take the chicken and not one of us."

(I've never taken one of their chickens. But there are enough hungry dogs, cats, and rats wandering the streets to convince the villagers that their offering truly protects them from my alleged hunger.)

One more thing Gauge didn't do after his grand-papá set sail. He reminds himself that there was no need, since he wasn't at the carpentry shop anyway. He thinks about Roux's proposal and is tempted to argue. Catching the Wolf is *his* job. But the jut of her chin tells him there will be no changing her mind.

As his initial shock wears off, he finds that he doesn't mind the idea. If he's being totally honest, there's a small part of him that is glad to have a part-ner, glad to have someone to help shoulder the burden. (I would have expected Roux to have more common sense than this—surely, she must realize the futility of attempting to catch me. But there's no reasoning with someone caught up in the throes of grief.)

Gauge realizes they have to work fast if they are to stand any chance of killing me before the ship—*the ship!*

He considers Roux, who spoons a mouthful of gruel and chews mindlessly. He hates to add to her

burden, but he has no choice. "There's one little problem," he says.

She lifts her head. "Only one?"

"Your father—how am I to board the ship?"

"I know the Captain, too," she says. "I'll get you on,
I swear. But we have to get rid of the Wolf first."

Gauge lets out a deep breath. The ship departs in
two days, which doesn't leave much time. He considers her chicken idea. He assumed he'd have to catch
me actually stealing a soul, but maybe Roux is onto
something. He's never seen me eat, but he can't say for
sure that I don't. I am, after all, a canine. A free meal
may well prove as irresistible as . . . Gauge thinks of
the moment I pulled his grandpapá's soul from his
old, wrinkled feet.

(That's one thing I'll be thrilled to leave behind.
I never had a problem with feet before—never gave
them much thought, truth be told. But there are only
so many stinky feet one can encounter before realizing
how disgusting they are. And it's not only the smell:
there's bunions, blisters, boils, corns, ingrown toenails,
and foot fungus to contend with, too.)

Gauge's anger swells.

"Where are we going to get our hands on a chicken?" he asks.

She stirs her gruel. "Same place as always. The market."

It's been several winters since Gauge visited the market. Images of narrow aisles, bright fabrics, rich scents, and glimmering fish dance in his head.

"I don't have any shells."

"I have what I received for the feathers. It should be enough."

Roux cleans her bowl and splashes water on her face. When Gauge returns from relieving himself, she's wearing a clean skirt and a shirt the color of a tart cherry. She presses a sheathed knife into his hands. "If you're going to hunt the Wolf, you're going to need this."

Gauge unsheathes the knife. The massive blade gleams by the light of the fire. The handle is carved of smooth white bone. He shakes his head. "I can't accept this."

Roux presses. "Please. My father would want you to have it."

Gauge can't remember the last time anybody

other than his grandpapá gifted him anything. Afraid of the heat rising behind his eyes, he busies himself tying the sheath around his waist. The leather pouch should make him feel stronger, more confident. Instead, it presses into his pain.

They hurry through the village, Roux leading the way. Gauge can't help but notice how different the streets feel today than they did even a few days earlier. Where the villagers usually call out greetings to each other and stop and catch up with friends and neighbors, today they all hurry about their business, their heads down. It's as if the entire village is cloaked in fear.

The boy's heart pounds out a warning. There are so many ways this could go wrong. He could be recognized. Or I could show up. He reminds himself that's what he *wants* to happen. But he wants it to be on his terms—not backed into a corner with the whole village watching.

As they near the market, Gauge's anxiety grows. He reaches under his tunic and grips the hilt of his knife.

They arrive at an arched doorway filled with colorful streams of fabric. Gauge is assaulted by a cacophony of sights and sounds. Venders yell, trying to attract customers. An astounding array of people push to and fro, trying to reach this stand or that. Dogs wander the crowded aisles, seeking fallen scraps of food.

"I didn't know there were this many people in all of Bouge," Gauge says.

"There aren't," Roux says. "We're the largest port in the area. People come from far and wide to trade."

A pang shoots through Gauge's heart as he watches a stout woman argue with a silver-haired vendor. What would his life have been like—what would *he* be like—if he'd grown up without the Wolf?

The boy sticks close to Roux, who expertly navigates through the market's many twists and turns. He's overwhelmed by the smells that fill the air— spiced nuts, warm bread, fresh fish of every kind. He stops to examine the many arms of what must be an octopus.

"You buying?" the vendor asks.

Gauge shakes his head.

"Then get moving."

Roux tugs him along. He's equal parts horrified

and fascinated by the array of fish that stare up at him with dead eyes. At one stand, rainbow-colored scales flash in the sunshine. Another brims with nothing but bulging eyeballs. He turns a corner and almost bumps into a stack of dead squirrels. He's seen the animals out the shop window, heard them running over the roof. He always thought of them as friends and imagined their chatter was meant for him.

The knife burns against his waist, a sharp reminder that he's constantly surrounded by death.

"Are you unwell?"

Gauge opens his eyes to find that he's stopped in the middle of an aisle. Roux's hand rests on his arm. He sucks in a deep breath, forces himself to speak. "Where are the chickens?"

"Almost there."

Indeed, it's only a few more turns before they arrive at a stand with a row of already-plucked poultry dangling by their legs.

"Well, if it isn't Woolsey the Blacksmith's daughter," a thin man with a bulbous red nose and heavily muscled arms sneers, removing a stick of jerky from his mouth.

"The late Blacksmith," Roux says, her chin dropping to her chest.

"He's been released, then? I was wondering how long he'd last."

Roux's eyes widen. "You knew he was ill?"

"Didn't take a Lord Mayor to figure that one out. Once he started coughing, it was only a matter of waiting for the wave to break." He studies Gauge. "Who's this?"

"Father's new Apprentice."

The Poulterer scrutinizes Gauge, who fights the urge to tug at his clothes. The wool is suddenly scratchy against his skin. (I always hated that feeling. Though I admit, I'd take wool over the fleas that plague me any day.)

"He'll be taking over the shop?"

"First thing tomorrow morning. Today we need to set out a chicken."

"I suppose you'll be wanting one of my birds?" The Poulterer tears off a bite of jerky, revealing stained teeth.

"Yes, please," Roux says.

"Four shells."

"Four shells!" Roux cries. "That's piracy!"

"No such thing."

"You've never charged me more than two."

The Poulterer shrugs. "Inflation."

"Very well, then, here are two." Roux hands over two iridescent shells. "Put me down for another two."

"Full payment only," the Poulterer says.

"But you've always given me credit. You know I'm good for it."

"I've always given your *father* credit. I can't be sure you two will pay up." He eyes Gauge. "This one looks shifty, if you ask me."

Gauge fixes his gaze on the stand next to them, where rows of salted herring wait for purchase.

"We'll settle up by the end of the month," Roux says. "He has plenty of my father's orders to fill."

She elbows Gauge.

"Ouch!" He rubs his side and then realizes the Poulterer is waiting for his assurance.

"That's right," Gauge says. "You'll get your shells."

The Poulterer tears off another hunk of jerky. "You're lucky I have a soft heart."

Gauge barely holds back a snort.

"End of month and no later." The Poulterer unties the smallest chicken. Gauge knows he should be grateful for any chicken at all, but suddenly everything he has endured stacks up in his mind, a teetering tower of emotion. It's too much—losing his grandpapá, the Blacksmith's death, Lord Mayor Vulpine, the Wolf, the shells they owe—all of it. And now this—the scrawniest, most pathetic chicken in all of Bouge. For four shells!

"Not that one," Gauge says firmly. "We'll take *that* one." He motions toward the largest chicken, its plump breasts nearly double the size of the one in the Poulterer's hand.

The Poulterer lets out a bark of surprised laughter. "What makes you think you have any say in the matter?"

"Four shells is far more than even the largest of your chickens is worth. But if you don't agree, we'll be happy to take our business elsewhere. You aren't the only Poulterer in the village."

Gauge has no idea if this is true or not, but he desperately hopes he's right.

The Poulterer scowls. Gauge juts his chin in the air, daring the man to push him.

After a fierce battle fought entirely with their eyes, the Poulterer switches the scrawny chicken in his hand for the plump chicken Gauge selected, muttering all the while about picky customers trying to squeeze him for every shell.

Gauge can hardly hide his gleeful smile as he reaches out to accept the chicken.

The Poulterer pulls the chicken out of reach. "One month," he growls.

"One month," Gauge promises, thinking that by then, either I will be dead or he will have died trying to kill me. Unless Lord Mayor Vulpine gets him first.

Chapter Ten

Gauge flops the dead chicken on the table. His mouth waters. Chicken was usually out of their budget, which included simple stews of potatoes, fish, and, in the summer, fresh vegetables.

But occasionally, when his grandpapá made a particularly big sale, or on the Darkest Day, when they both needed a reminder that winter wouldn't last forever, the old man would go out and bring back a chicken. He and Gauge would scald and pluck and roast it, filling their entire home with the delicious smell of carrots and rosemary. They'd have fresh meat for days after, and then soup made from its rich broth.

The boy reminds himself that this chicken isn't for eating.

"Do you think this will work?" he asks.

"Dunno," Roux says, stoking the fire. "Do you?"

"It has to," the boy says. He rests his hand on the handle of his newly acquired knife, thinking how best to attack me. Go for the neck, perhaps? Or would he be better off aiming for the heart? He scratches his head, wondering where exactly a Wolf's heart is located.

(It's right under my rib cage, same as his.)

He decides to go for my neck. He rubs a clammy hand on his pants, feeling as though night may never arrive (they believe there's no sense in setting the chicken out during the day, wolves being mostly nocturnal and all). There has to be something he can do to hurry things along. "Here, Wolf, Wolf, Wolf."

Roux whirls from the fire. "What are you doing?"

"Trying to summon the Wolf," Gauge says, fighting the heat in his cheeks.

"It's not a cat," Roux says. "And anyway, I thought the idea was to catch her off guard?"

The boy runs a hand through his hair. He doesn't know if it's even possible to catch me off guard. And he'd rather face me now than worry about it all day.

He sinks down on the Blacksmith's bed and squeezes his eyes shut. If he concentrates hard enough, if he can draw an exact picture of me in his mind, he can't help but think that maybe I'll appear.

He opens his eyes to find Roux scowling. He grips his knife, thinking—hoping—that I might walk in.

A short time later, there's a knock on the front door, quick and firm.

Gauge dives for the back door. Roux motions for him to calm. "We don't know who it is."

The boy wonders if, instead of calling me, he called Lord Mayor Vulpine's Guards. He hovers by the door as Roux hurries to the front. Her soft footsteps are ominous in the otherwise silent room. The front door squeaks open.

"Can I help you?" Roux asks.

Gauge has the feeling she's speaking extra loudly for his benefit. He strains but can't hear the answer.

She speaks again. "What's this?"

A pause. "You can't possibly expect me to—110 shells? I can't come up with that!"

A longer pause. "You'll have to give me some time. Can I make payments?"

"Fine." Her voice is gruff. "Thank you for coming by."

The door slams.

She stomps back in the living room.

"What is it?" Gauge asks.

She drops a bill onto the table.

The boy gasps. "One hundred and ten shells for the vessel?"

"Due by the month's end."

"But that's, there's . . ." Gauge is at a loss for words. First the Healer's bill, then the chicken, now this. "That's not fair."

(Fair or not, the Blacksmith didn't make arrangements for his vessel prior to his passing. One can hardly blame the Vessel-maker for sending along one of his finer designs. He is, after all, a businessperson.)

"There's no way I can pay this," Roux says, clutching the bill. "Not even if Yanis fills all of Father's orders."

The boy moves to her side and rests a hand on her shoulders. "We'll figure something out."

"Easy for you to say," she says. "The Vessel-maker wouldn't know where to collect payment from you even if he wanted to."

The reminder that Gauge can't return home pierces his stomach, gutting him.

"I'm sorry," Roux says. "I shouldn't have . . ."

Gauge gives a quick nod, accepting her apology. But silence falls like a fisherman's net, trapping each of them in their own miserable thoughts.

Darkness saunters toward them, taking more time than it has any right to claim. Gauge plans to put the chicken out the minute the moon crawls into the sky, but Roux convinces him to wait until right before bed, when the streets are well and truly empty.

"The Wolf isn't going to be prancing around where anybody can see it," she says. (Since Gauge is the only one who can see me, this is hardly a concern. But the girl is grieving, so she must be forgiven for her lack of sense.)

Gauge bites back a surly response and fingers the knife at his side. This is it. Tonight he'll finally have the chance to do right by his grandpapá's memory. And be rid of me once and for all.

It's near midnight when he places the chicken outside. He's acutely aware of the missing head, the empty chest cavity, the rubbery wings that used to be lined with feathers.

"May you sail in peace," he mumbles. There is so much he doesn't know. Do chickens go to the Sea-in-the-Sky? They have wings and feathers that might get them there, but what about other animals? Dogs? *Wolves?*

The boy's throat turns dry and scratchy. He recalls meeting me down at the shore. He can't imagine what kind of offer I might have for him, but he doesn't want any part of it. *Stay away from the Wolf,* his grandpapá said.

"I'm going to take care of it, Grandpapá," Gauge whispers.

He leaves the door ajar for an easy exit the moment I appear, squats at a window, and lifts the shade enough to reveal the street, wondering which direction I'll come from.

Across the doorway, Roux peeks out the other window and then slides to the floor.

"You should get some sleep," Gauge whispers.

"I'm not going anywhere."

"I can manage on my own," he says.

"Sure you can. Like you did when the Guards stopped us?"

"I would have been fine," the boy insists, knowing he's as full as a puffer fish.

She doesn't budge.

The boy is torn between the urge to strangle her and the warm ribbon of gratitude wrapping itself around his chest. There's comfort in her smooth, rhythmic breathing, in knowing that when I arrive, he won't have to face me alone.

As silence settles around them, he thinks back to when his grandpapá taught him to carve a slender twig into a flower. If he had his folding knife and a branch, he'd cut away the bark and peel thin layers from the stem, allowing it to curl into delicate petals. He imagines tucking one behind Roux's ear.

Focus, Gauge reminds himself. *You have a Wolf to kill.*

The seconds tick by.

The boy has almost given up hope. His head droops and his eyelids are growing heavy when he hears the sound of footsteps on the street. He sits up straight, suddenly alert. Roux raises her finger to her lips to remind him to remain quiet as she pulls up the shade ever so slightly. Gauge unsheathes his knife, clutches it in a tight fist. His heart pounds in his ears.

A movement appears on the street. A drunken villager lurches past them. He stops to relieve himself against the shop's wall. Gauge's grip on the knife tightens as his frustration surges.

Roux drops the shade and yawns, but the boy knows better than to encourage her to go to bed. They sit for the better part of the night, watching, waiting. Again the boy's eyelids grow heavy. He blinks rapidly, attempting to stay awake. A sharp blow hits his ribs. "Ouch!" he whisper-shouts. "What'd you do that for?"

"You fell asleep."

"Did not."

"Do you normally snore when you're wide awake?"

Gauge can't think of an answer. He shifts uncomfortably on the floor. A sharp breeze sneaks in through the crack in the door. "What if the Wolf doesn't come?"

"Then we'll make a new plan in the morning," Roux says. "For now, we have to get through tonight."

Get through tonight. Even though it's only been three days since his grandpapá's death, Gauge feels like all he has done is try to *get through*. Every moment, every breath without the old man is a stabbing pain in his chest.

Gauge closes his eyes, remembers his grandpapá's firm grip as he taught the boy to cut through a plank, helped him hold the saw straight and steady. Never again will he feel the old man's warm breath on his cheek, hear his cheerful whistle.

Gauge forces his eyes open, refusing to let grief pull him under. The best he can do is to push his grief aside, try to face each moment as it comes.

Beside him, Roux folds and unfolds the edge of her tunic. She isn't having any easier time of it, even if she is putting on a brave face. He wonders: What is it about death, exactly, that makes living feel so hard?

Chapter Eleven

If I'm ever to get through to the boy, I need him to stop clinging to his grandpapá's last words, to continue doubting everything he's ever been told. Maybe I can offer him a clue, something to make sure he keeps searching for the truth.

As I approach the sleeping boy, the crackling fire casts a warm glow over his face. After he and Roux gave up luring me with the chicken, they brought it inside and dropped it into the cooking pot with a bit of garlic and rosemary before collapsing in their respective beds and falling into a sore, defeated sleep.

He looks so peaceful, so free of his pain and anger, that it takes my breath away. But no. I can't let myself develop feelings for this boy. I'm doing what's best for him. For both of us. For the entire country.

I shudder, imagining all of us spending eternity in the Bog. Though the villagers believe the place is terrorized by Voyants, the truth is every bit as bad: souls that end up in the Bog are stuck languishing amongst the foul stench of decaying moss and stagnant groundwater.

I shove my muzzle under his pillow, feeling for the two halves of the mirror he tucked there for safekeeping. If the boy only pays it a little attention, he'll notice that the mirror is broken down the middle in a straight line. Surely, he'll realize how strange, how unnatural, that is.

He snorts and rolls over.

I freeze and then use my mouth to ever-so-slowly slide the pieces toward me. Intent on arranging them so he will see the two perfect halves when he wakes up, I flip one half over so the glass faces up. The other half is between my teeth when his eyes flicker open.

This is bad. This is very bad. Now he'll trust me less than ever.

"You!" he says, scrambling away from me and

fumbling for his knife. His jaw is set with grim determination.

I drop the mirror onto the mattress and disappear.

Gauge sits still, sucking in deep, frightened breaths. He doesn't know why I was there, can't imagine what interest I might have in the mirror. He picks up the pieces gingerly, holding them as though they might bite. They are a bit slobbery, but otherwise, he can't see anything special about them.

He stays huddled in bed until Roux finally stirs.

"What is it?" Roux asks, noting his pale, drawn face. "What's the matter?"

The boy tucks the pieces of mirror in his pocket, promising himself that if I come for them again he'll be ready, and shakes his head. He doesn't know what I'm up to, but he won't give Roux another reason to worry.

They pull the chicken from the pot and sit down at the table.

"We need a new plan," Roux says.

Gauge takes a bite but hardly notices the moist, flavorful meat. With the ship leaving tomorrow, time is running out. "I've been thinking the same thing."

Roux wrinkles her nose. "Don't talk with food in your mouth. It's revolting."

Heat rushes to Gauge's cheeks (for approximately the hundredth time since meeting her. The boy really needs to get a grip on himself). He finishes chewing and swallows. "Baiting the Wolf didn't help. We're going to have to track it."

"How?" Roux asks.

"What if we don't track it directly? What if we figure out where it's going to be and wait for it there?"

"An ambush?"

The boy nods.

Roux thinks. "Are you saying we need to find someone ready to set sail? How are we going to do that?"

"The easiest way would be to follow Nicoline the Healer."

"But that could take days. Who knows when one of her patients will go? Besides, we don't know if the Wolf comes for everyone who sets sail."

Gauge bristles. "Well, we can't follow the Steward. She'd recognize me faster than a pelican diving for dinner."

He jumps up. "I know!"

Roux cocks her head.

"Follow me. I'll explain on the way."

Ruben the Vessel-maker's shop is on the other side of the village. The windows are freshly washed and a large sign with finely printed letters hangs from the front.

Gauge and Roux saunter past, noting the small lobby featuring two thickly cushioned chairs, a gilded table offering an assortment of nuts and cheeses, and a painting on the wall of the Sea-in-the-Sky lit with the light of a thousand lanterns.

The painting is a reminder of how Gauge's grandpapá never made it to the Sea-in-the-Sky, never had a chance to light a lantern. The boy's heart sinks like an anchor, but he forces himself to continue on, putting one foot in front of the next.

They cross the street and reverse directions, confirming that the lobby is empty.

"Let's check behind the shop," Gauge murmurs. They follow the muck-filled alley to a yard teeming with stacks of sawn lumber. The sounds of hammering and sawing ring from inside. A barrel-chested man unloads wood from a sturdy wagon.

Gauge and Roux slip behind a pile of wood and make their way to the narrow gap between the Vessel-maker's building and the one next to it. An open window reveals a large workshop teeming with activity. The smell of sawdust fills Gauge's nose.

Boys and girls from approximately twelve winters to several winters older—all Apprentices, Gauge guesses—build vessels of different sizes. The boy's heart squeezes as he recognizes many of the same tools from his grandpapá's shop.

Some vessels are plain and some are brightly painted, while others feature detailed carvings of everything from elaborate scrolls to fish to forest animals. Like the crew that attended his grandpapá, the Apprentices have skin that ranges from light to dark, but they are all dressed in white and most wear aprons to protect their clothing.

"Perfect," he whispers. "They crew for the Steward."

Boisterous laughter comes from a second-floor window above their heads. Both children freeze. A voice Gauge doesn't recognize floats through the air. "Avril, can I offer you a cup of tea?"

"Don't mind if I do," Lord Mayor Vulpine's booming voice answers.

Gauge and Roux look at each other, startled. They've never heard anyone address Lord Mayor Vulpine by his first name before—had never given thought to the fact that he might have one.

Lord Mayor Vulpine continues, "Tell me, how is the death business these days?"

"Quick, give me a lift," Gauge says, scooting to an oak tree that stretches from the ground, reaching for what little sun it can find.

"No, Gauge. It's too risky."

"Come on—I'll only take a peek."

With a sigh, Roux folds her hands together. The boy steps into them and pulls himself up onto a branch, holding in a grunt as the rough bark bites his skin. He's never climbed a tree before and doesn't have a proper feel for it. But he's awed by the tree's strength, by its power. So different from the milled wood delivered to the shop. He stops to run his fingers over a knot, imagining it as part of a tabletop. A burl twists a branch above his head. The branch shoots into the sky at an awkward angle.

"What happened to you?" Gauge whispers, wondering what secrets the tree holds.

His hesitation gives Roux's misgivings time to grow. "Gauge," she whispers. "Come back down."

Gauge startles and nearly falls. A sturdy limb stretches out, reaching for the open window. Buds cluster together at the tips of the tree's branches.

"Don't do it," Roux pleads.

Gauge lowers his body down on the branch, wraps his legs around it, and inches out until he can peer in the window. Lord Mayor Vulpine and a man Gauge guesses must be the Vessel-maker sit in the finest room the boy has ever seen. Thick rugs cover the floor and tapestries of beautiful sunsets line the walls.

Both men rest in ornate chairs covered with floral carvings Gauge recognizes as his grandpapá's work. They sip tea from cups painted with fleurs-de-lis. The sweet, slightly woody smell of chamomile wafts toward the boy. Lord Mayor Vulpine's intricately carved cane rests on the arm of his chair, its snaked head hissing at Gauge as if attempting to warn him away.

The Vessel-maker's mahogany skin lacks luster. He is painfully thin, his every feature pointed. His bony fingers are adorned with heavy gold rings.

"How are you and your sister getting along?" the Vessel-maker asks.

Lord Mayor Vulpine waves him off. "She and I will never see eye-to-eye. She doesn't understand the burden of my position—too busy trying to save everyone she touches."

The men chuckle.

Gauge didn't know Lord Mayor Vulpine had a sister.

"And what of the Voyant?" the Vessel-maker asks. "Any news of his whereabouts?"

Lord Mayor Vulpine shakes his head. "It's maddening. The boy disappeared into thin air. It can only be witchery." He holds out his cup. "I wouldn't turn down a nip, if you offered."

Although a teapot rests on the table, the Vessel-maker pulls a glass flask from his breast pocket. Uncorking the lid, he pours a generous serving of amber liquid into Lord Mayor Vulpine's cup and then his own.

"What do you suppose the boy is up to?" The Vessel-maker takes a long, greedy swig.

Anger burns inside the boy, starting in his chest and spreading outward. He's not up to anything. He only wants to get rid of me and then escape the village with his life intact.

"Can't quite figure it out. But he's dangerous, I'll tell you that much. The boy had no sooner spotted the Wolf than my dear wife set sail."

"But if the boy were trouble, surely he would have done more damage after all this time?" the Vessel-maker asks.

"Not with the old man around—kept the boy in line. Now that he's gone . . ." Lord Mayor Vulpine leans forward. "The very first thing the boy did after the old man set sail was call the Wolf to the Wharves."

Gauge snorts. Lord Mayor Vulpine and the Vessel-maker turn to the window. The boy jerks back.

The sudden movement throws him off balance. His body lurches to the side. He tries to correct himself, but it's too late—he teeters and then falls, crashing to the ground with a resounding thud.

Roux lunges to help, but Gauge is already jumping to his feet. They flatten themselves against the wall in time to hear the Vessel-maker say, "One of my crew tripping over themselves, most likely. I swear they all have two left feet."

The men laugh and Gauge breathes a sigh of relief as he checks himself for injuries. His hands are scraped and his hip is sore, but otherwise he's no worse for the wear.

"Come on." Roux tugs at his arm, guiding him back to the workshop window.

Three boys and one girl, all sturdy and somber, select a vessel from a stack in the back of the room. They load the vessel on a cart, exit through the back door, and clomp down the alley, mud collecting on their heavy clogs.

Roux and Gauge slink toward the alley, where they straighten and attempt to appear as though they are only out for a stroll. (No one in their right minds would stroll through an alley in Bouge, but the crew is intent on their task and doesn't think to question this strange behavior.)

Gauge senses Roux sneaking glances at him as if judging whether or not he is upset. He pretends he doesn't notice. The truth is, he's more than a little rattled. Knowing they believe he's a Voyant is one thing. Hearing Lord Mayor Vulpine speak of Gauge in such strong terms—his insistence that Gauge caused Mistress Vulpine's death, that the boy is out to hurt more people . . . Gauge's anger returns. It's not fair—he didn't ask to be a Voyant, doesn't want to be one. And he's not evil.

At least he doesn't think he is. Gauge's conviction falters. What if Lord Mayor Vulpine is right? There is Mistress Vulpine, and then his grandpapá. And is it really coincidence that the Blacksmith set sail right after Gauge's arrival? What if it is all his fault?

Roux keeps pace beside him. The boy's stomach churns. If it's true what Lord Mayor Vulpine says, then she's in tremendous danger.

No. Gauge grits his teeth. He doesn't know why all of this is happening, but it's not his fault. Anyway, he's going to fix it. And Roux is going to be fine.

Ahead of them, three members of the crew have shaken off their serious mood. They laugh and joke as they push the empty vessel through the village. The fourth member, a boy Gauge's age but stockier, with freckled skin and clay-colored hair, is sullen and withdrawn.

"What's skinning your fish?" one of the crew asks him.

"The Vessel-maker denied my request for a transfer."

The girl asks, "Why would you want a transfer? We don't have it so bad."

Gauge strains but doesn't hear the boy's response. (It hardly matters, but I can see you are curious. The boy longs to be a fisherman. He loathes spending most of his time inside, but he's bound to the Vessel-maker for seven winters. The Vessel-maker certainly isn't going to give up free help simply because one of his workers isn't happy.)

They exchange a few more sentences and then the boy mutters, "It's such a joke, the time we put into these vessels. It's not as if it matters."

Gauge and Roux share confused glances.

The crew slows and then stops in front of a bakery, where a cage full of pigeons rests on a cart. The Steward—busy hanging a fishing net on the door of the bakery—greets them in a clipped voice. Three deaths in five days isn't unusual in a place as big as Bouge, but she's still on edge after her close encounter with the Voyant.

Gauge and Roux hang back and pretend to study

the wares displayed in a Cheese-maker's window while the crew unloads the vessel and disappears inside.

Gauge and Roux move closer.

"Well?" Roux says. "Is the Wolf here?"

The boy sniffs the air. Nothing. He inches forward.

"Not too close," Roux cautions. "The Steward might spot you when she comes out."

A whiff of something wild and pungent catches Gauge's attention.

(Although I can't be sure what form I'll be in once I reach the Woods Beyond, I certainly hope it's human. The first thing I'm going to do after smothering my daughter with love is have a good long wash and scrub at my skin until I've done away with this odor for good.)

The smell fades. Unaware that I came and went through the back door, Gauge nears the front of the shop. "There's nothing," he says, running a frustrated hand over his head. "I'm pretty sure the Wolf was here, but she's gone now."

"Come on," Roux says, tugging at him. "Let's get out of here."

As the two move down the street, Gauge huffs. "It's not going to work, following the crew—we'll always arrive too late."

"We're going to have to follow a Healer," Roux says.

"That will take forever. The ship leaves tomorrow."

Roux reaches for a strand of hair, sees him looking, and itches her scalp instead. "Do you have any better ideas?"

Gauge wants to argue. Not because he disagrees—because he needs to release some of the emotions swirling in his chest. But the friendship is too new, both of them too fragile. And there aren't any other options. He sucks in a deep breath. "Fine," he says. "Let's go."

They debate whether to hunt down a Healer who won't recognize them but decide to risk being spotted in order to save time. After arriving at the square, they plant themselves in a mostly dry spot under a large tree with sprawling arms that stretch out over their heads. Evergreen shrubs shelter them from view. Seated with their backs against the tree trunk, they are able to keep watch on Nicoline the Healer's front door without worrying that she (or Master Vulpine, although they aren't sure if he's already returned home) might see them.

Gauge picks a blade of dry grass and runs it through his fingers.

"What do you think he meant, that the vessels don't matter?" He fights to keep his voice from shaking.

Roux thinks out loud. "He couldn't mean that the vessels don't matter. He must have meant that the designs on the vessels don't matter—that they are a waste of time."

The boy considers her words. It's possible she's right. But his earlier questions fester under his skin. What about the Healer's easy dismissal of shaving? The Steward's lack of concern when Roux forgot a lantern? The fact that his grandpapá didn't get any oars? He can't shake the feeling that there's something big he's missing.

(It's all I can do not to nip at the boy's ears for failing to recognize the clue I left him. But at least he's thinking.)

The boy ties the blade of grass in a knot, tugging the ends until they rip apart.

The Healer's door opens. A long, flowing skirt

wraps around her waist and a thin, wispy jacket nearly reaches the ground. Although her clothes are fancier than the last time they saw her, she still carries her healing basket.

Gauge and Roux jump to their feet. But instead of leaving the square, the Healer hurries around it, stopping at Lord Mayor Vulpine's home.

"What's she doing there?" Roux asks.

"Maybe he's sick," Gauge says, conflicted by how happy the thought makes him. He wrestles with himself over whether he should feel guilty for wishing ill upon someone who wants him dead.

A plump, middle-aged woman they assume is Lord Mayor Vulpine's Keeper opens the door. After a short conversation, she disappears. Lord Mayor Vulpine fills the doorway.

"He doesn't look sick," Roux says. "Anyway, you just saw him and he was fine."

Gauge can't argue either point.

Lord Mayor Vulpine and the Healer exchange cordial greetings, and then Lord Mayor Vulpine drops a fistful of what appears to be shells into the Healer's hand. She tucks the shells in her bag and departs.

"What do you think that was about?" Gauge asks.

"No idea," Roux says.

Staying at a careful distance, they follow the Healer through the village. She stops at a long, low building the boy hasn't seen in several winters.

Rope, the sign says.

Gauge visited this place with his grandpapá as a small child. As the Healer knocks on the door and is granted admittance, he thinks back to a drafty shop filled with ropes of various sizes hanging from the walls, some half-finished, some ready and waiting for customers in need. The Rope-maker was gruff but kind. Gauge searches his memory for her name, Elayna? Eloise? Elise! Elise the Rope-maker. After his grandpapá completed his business, she slipped Gauge a hard candy whose sour shell hid a sweet center.

"Let's go around the back," Roux says.

They edge up to the living room at the back of the shop. Darkness has settled around them and heavy clouds block the lanterns above. Bright light shines from two windows, one on each side of the building. Gauge and Roux tuck themselves in the shadows on one side and peer through the glass.

The living room contains a table and benches, a hearth, and a wide bed tucked in the corner. A woman he doesn't know kneels over the Rope-maker. The unknown woman's thick black hair is held back by a colorful scarf. The Rope-maker's straw-colored hair is matted against her flushed face.

"She's got the fever," Roux whispers.

The boy knows he should be relieved—this means I will soon be on my way. But his chest tightens at the thought of death claiming yet another life. It isn't fair—watching good people pass while others—like Lord Mayor Vulpine—continue living.

The Rope-maker moans and writhes, obviously trying to settle her aching body into a comfortable position. The unknown woman tugs a blanket up to the Rope-maker's chin, presses a cloth against her forehead, and strokes her cheek.

Gauge averts his eyes. "My mother was taken by the fever."

"I'm sorry."

He shrugs, not sure why he brought it up. "I don't remember her."

"That's terrible," Roux says.

"Why does it matter?"

"I mean no offense, it's . . . well, I miss my mother more than anything, but at least I have my memories. I can't imagine what it would be like, not knowing her at all."

Gauge considers her words, thinks of how hard it is without his grandpapá. She's right—it's the memories of the time he spent with the old man, the love that shined from his eyes, that keeps Gauge going. When he thinks of his mother, there's nothing more than a faint stirring, a distant curiosity.

Perhaps if he had something that belonged to her, he might feel more of a connection? A shawl that still carried a hint of her scent, gloves that hugged her hands—even a pot or pan she used might offer some clue to who she was, give him something to anchor her in his mind.

At least he has what his grandpapá told him about his mother—that's more than he can say about his father. His grandpapá claimed the man's identity was a secret Gauge's mother took to the Sea-in-the-Sky. (The boy would be sadly disappointed if he knew the truth—his father had no interest in raising a child. In any case, a boating accident claimed him before Gauge was born.)

The boy's thoughts turn back to his grandpapá. A hard lump of panic forms in his throat as the boy realizes he still doesn't know what kind of fish was his grandpapá's favorite. How many other things does he not know or will he forget over the winters?

He recalls stumbling and falling on the corner of a chair, the flash of pain and the dark mark that appeared on his thigh soon after. What if memories are like bruises—strong in the beginning but eventually fading away to nothing?

No. He won't let himself forget a single thing about his grandpapá. It's the remembering—the relationship and the love they shared—that's most important.

Still, the fresh air filling his lungs, the sound of dogs barking in the distance, Roux's breathing beside him all make him think about how much he missed, hidden away in the shop. Sadness softens the panic in his throat. The life of a hermit crab is fine if you're a hermit crab, but humans need each other. He's tempted to reach for Roux's hand but instead rubs his thumb along the metal heart in his pocket and peeks through the window.

The Rope-maker's hair falls in her face. Gauge expects the Healer to shave it off. Instead, she pulls it back and fastens it. The Rope-maker moans. The unknown woman lifts the Rope-Maker's head, encourages her to drink. The Rope-maker tries to swallow but almost immediately spews bile into a bucket resting by the bed.

"Eeew." Roux and Gauge groan and pull back.

They lean against the wall for several minutes, waiting quietly.

"Have you figured out yet what you are going to do when all this is over?" Roux finally asks. "You know, in Figeac?"[6]

"Figeac?" Gauge has been so focused on finding the Wolf that he hasn't thought about the ship's destination. Grandpapá occasionally talked about the country's warm air, fresh fruit, and vegetables year-round. He can't quite picture how he'll build a life in a place so different from Bouge, but he'll have to make a go of it somehow.

---

6. *It's FEE-jack. But you probably already knew that, didn't you?*

"I suppose I'll try to get on with a Carpenter."

The thought makes him both happy and sad. He pictures himself behind a counter, greeting his first customer. It won't be the same without Grandpapá by his side, but at least he'll be honoring the old man's work, carrying on the family tradition.

In the distance, angry waves roar.

"What about you?" he asks.

"I suppose Yanis will run the shop."

"Is he a Master?"

"No, but he's been with my father five winters. Two more winters and he could have applied for Master himself."

"Will anyone give him business?"

"We'll have to see."

"What will you do?"

"The same thing I've always done, I guess. Make deliveries, gather feathers."

"Why didn't your father train you to follow in his footsteps?"

"He wanted to. But I never saw metal like he did— as something to be shaped and molded, like a puzzle."

That's exactly how Gauge feels about carpentry.

He loves everything about it—the smell of freshly cut wood, picturing something in his mind and then watching it take shape, the satisfaction that comes each time he puts the finishing touch on a piece of furniture. He's surprised to hear the Blacksmith felt the same about his trade.

He thinks back to the contentment on the man's face when they worked on the heart. The boy recalls the twisted oak he climbed at the Vessel-maker's, compares it to the sturdy chestnut at the Wharves. Passions must be like trees—they come in all different shapes and sizes.

"Besides, I hate the smoke and noise. We thought that by collecting feathers maybe I'd have a shot at being named Steward someday."

"Would you like that?"

Roux traces a brick on the wall. "I thought so, but now . . . Dealing with death all the time . . ." When she looks up, her eyes are filled with questions. "I feel like the Steward should have known more about the Wolf."

Gauge has been thinking the same thing. How can the Steward be sure she's releasing souls when she doesn't know when they are missing?

"I'm not sure anymore," Roux continues. "About anything."

Gauge pities her. Not because of her confusion about the Steward—he feels exactly the same. But when all this is over, at least he'll have carpentry.

"What would you do if you could do anything?" he asks.

She crosses her arms and hugs them to her chest. "I want to do something that helps people. That really makes a difference in their lives."

"Like what?"

Before she can answer, an anguished cry breaks their conversation. "No!"

Inside, the unknown woman has thrown herself across the Rope-maker's body. The dead woman's hair clings to her sweaty head. The boy draws his knife from its sheath. "It's time."

He moves toward the back of the building. Roux steps on his heel.

"What are you doing?" he asks.

"Coming to help."

"You don't have a weapon. Please, let me do this."

He rounds the corner and crouches beside the back door, his hand shaking as he raises his knife above his head, preparing to strike.

The door opens. The Healer exits, her basket resting on her arm. She tucks what Gauge is certain are shells into her pocket. The boy slips the blade behind his back and tries to fade into the shadows.

"You're lucky I didn't mistake you for a thief," she says. "Come out of the dark."

Gauge considers running, but there's no sense in it. Not when she's already spotted him. Besides, she sounds more curious than angry.

"Why are you trailing me?"

"What? We're not." He glances back to where Roux peeks around the corner, little more than a shadow to anyone who doesn't know she's there, and attempts to correct himself. "I'm not."

"I saw you back at the square." She squints into the dark. "You and Roux. Don't bother denying it. Now tell me what you're up to."

The boy suspects he's missing my appearance inside. His frustration teeters like a rocking boat and then capsizes. "I don't have time for this. I have a Wolf to catch."

He slaps his hand over his mouth.

From around the corner, Roux groans.

The Healer nearly drops her basket. She recovers and steps closer to Gauge as if trying to read the truth in his face. "A Wolf?"

She suspected from the beginning that this was the boy Lord Mayor Vulpine was searching for. But up to this point, she wasn't convinced that I was real, and she didn't really believe that there was any such thing as a Voyant. In fact, part of her wondered if all the Wolf business was a story made up by the Lord Mayors to keep people living in fear. Now that she knows the truth, she's curious. She's spent too much time with death to fear it.

"Not that I know anything about the Wolf," Gauge says in a rush. "I don't. I'm only trying to help, since Lord Mayor Vulpine says it's here in the village."

"Mmmm," the Healer says thoughtfully.

Gauge gulps. "Don't tell him about me, please."

"You don't have to worry about that. I've never been inclined to tell Avril anything, and I'm not about to start now. But I am curious—what are you going to do with the Wolf if you find it?"

Gauge tips his chin in the air. "I'm going to kill it."

The Healer's pointed eyebrows jump up. "Are you now?"

"I am," Gauge says determinedly.

"Well, I wish you good luck with that."

"You don't think I can do it?"

The Healer pauses as if searching for the right words. "I don't know what to think," she finally says. "But I can't help but wonder if your anger is misguided."

"Who else should I be angry at?" He thinks of how she didn't shave the Rope-maker's head, hears the wailing coming from inside the Rope-maker's home. "You? Pretending you can help people when all you do is take their money?"

"I'm sure it looks that way to you. But I do what I can and offer comfort where I can't."

Gauge bristles at her calm demeanor. "Aren't you scared the Wolf is going to get you?"

"I'm afraid of a good many things," she says. "Being stolen by a magical Wolf isn't one of them."

She opens her mouth. For a moment, Gauge thinks she's going to continue the conversation. Instead she says, "Now if you'll excuse me, I have to notify Mistress Charbonneaux that she's needed."

She disappears down the alley, her gauzy jacket fluttering behind her.

Chapter Twelve

While Gauge and Roux carry on with the Healer in the back, I pad toward the front of the shop and let myself in. Having no interest in a confrontation, I extract the Rope-maker's soul and exit the way I came. My joints ache terribly, no doubt a symptom of my advanced age. A faint buzzing rings in my ears— my hearing must be going, too. I fight images of my dilapidated body curled in a heap, my soul sinking to the Bog. I smell the damp rot, feel the misery of such an existence.

Gauge knows nothing of my worry but shoulders plenty of his own. After the Healer disappears into the dark, he and Roux rush back to the side window. Inside, the scene appears much the same as the last time he looked, but the boy detects my scent. He rests his forehead against the wall. "We missed her."

He sinks down on a stack of firewood.

Roux settles next to him but doesn't attempt to speak. Truthfully, she doesn't have any comfort to offer, not gutted as she is by her own grief.

The boy notices she's shivering, realizes he's shivering, too. He can't remember the last time he felt warm—really, truly warm. His grandpapá's death turned him into one of the icebergs he heard about from across the sea, freezing him from the inside out. He opens and closes his fingers, trying to generate some heat.

Questions from earlier soar and swoop in his mind like a conspiracy of ravens searching for a meal. How come the Steward did so little for his grandpapá? How come she didn't care if Roux brought a lantern? And what about the Healer—she didn't bother cutting the Rope-maker's hair. It's almost as if—

"That's it!" He jumps up.

"What?" Roux scrambles to her feet.

"I don't think it's real," he says.

"What isn't real?"

"The Release." (Finally, the boy is using his head! Now we're getting somewhere.)

Roux steps back. "You think the Steward is faking it?"

He runs through the evidence.

"Why would she do something like that?"

Gauge shrugs. "Shells, maybe? If there's no Release, she doesn't earn a living."

Roux twirls her hair around her finger. "I'm not saying you're right. But if you are onto something, do you think the Healer knows?"

"She has to. That's why she didn't care if my grand-papá's hair got cut. She didn't cut the Rope-maker's, either."

"But she doesn't get anything from Releases," Roux says doubtfully. "Plus, when you talked to her just now, she sounded surprised to hear the Wolf is real."

"Or maybe we *thought* she was surprised to hear the Wolf is real. Maybe she was actually surprised that I'm tracking it."

"I guess," Roux says, unconvinced. "But I still don't see what she gets out of pretending."

Gauge runs his hand through his hair. "It has to be some type of scheme."

Chirping crickets fill the silence between them.

Gauge punches a victorious fist in the air. "I've got it!"

"Shhh," Roux says, glancing at the window.

Gauge cringes, waiting to see if he attracted attention. When no one comes to the window, he continues in a hushed voice that trembles with excitement. "The Healer knows the Release is fake. But she keeps her mouth shut, the Steward makes a living, and the Wolf gets all the souls she wants. In return, the Wolf leaves the Steward and the Healer alone." (I can't help the sigh that escapes me. Perhaps the boy isn't as clever as I thought.)

"That explains why the Healer said she wasn't worried about the Wolf."

"Exactly!"

"But wait a minute," Roux says. "The Wolf doesn't need the Steward or the Healer's cooperation to take all the souls she wants. Besides, they can't talk to the Wolf. Not unless one of them is a Voyant."

Gauge frowns.

"Anyway, they wouldn't dare do this behind Lord Mayor Vulpine's back," Roux says.

Gauge's mind whirls. It's like he's holding a half-done carving in his hand and can't quite see how to finish.

He remembers the Healer stopping at Lord Mayor Vulpine's house earlier, the shells he slipped into her hand. "What if he's in on it? What if he controls the Wolf?"

Roux gasps. "You think Lord Mayor Vulpine is a Voyant?"

"Think about it—blaming others takes the attention off him."

Roux's eyes widen. "That's why he's so eager to pin his wife's death on you."

"And why he's so desperate—he has to get rid of me before I tell on him."

"It explains everything," Roux says. "The Steward, the Healer . . . all of it."

Gauge and Roux stare at each other, each silently poking and prodding their theory for holes, hardly able to believe what they uncovered but certain they're right. (I can't decide whether to laugh or cry, though I shouldn't be surprised by their logic. People can talk themselves into nearly anything once they set their minds to it. On second thought, maybe this isn't so bad—Gauge may be setting himself up for disappointment, but if he continues down this path, it won't be long before he's ready to hear the truth.)

"We've got to stop them," Roux says.

Gauge shakes his head. "Lord Mayor Vulpine is too big. Too powerful. We have to focus on finding the Wolf."

"I don't care how powerful he is," Roux spits out. "We can't let him get away with this."

Gauge is surprised by the intensity of Roux's anger, but she's right. They can't let Lord Mayor Vulpine continue terrorizing the village.

They sink back down and sit in silence.

"Maybe there's a way to catch two fish with one net," Gauge says slowly.

"How's that?"

"We haven't had any luck finding the Wolf on our own."

"So?"

"So what if we get Lord Mayor Vulpine to help?"

Roux snorts. "Sure. We'll pay him a visit and ask him to turn the Wolf over."

"I didn't say he'd do it willingly. We'll have to find some kind of proof. Something to show everyone he's a Voyant. Once the villagers know his secret, they'll force him to help us."

Gauge jumps to his feet once again. "After the Wolf is dead, the villagers will have to pardon me. This is it—my chance to clear my name. I'm not going to have to leave on the ship!"

"And Lord Mayor Vulpine will finally get what he has coming," Roux says. "But how are we going to prove it?"

Gauge lets out a long breath. "There must be a way."

Footsteps echo in the alley. Gauge and Roux press themselves farther into the shadows.

A familiar voice cuts through the dark. "This'll be the place."

Gauge and Roux watch through the window as the grieving woman grants the Steward and her crew admittance. The new crew, this time two boys and two girls, grunts as they set the vessel by the bed.

Gauge frowns. Why would they have made the vessel out of beech? It's inexpensive but heavy—surely no good for a trip to the Sea-in-the-Sky. He shakes his head, reminding himself that the Release is fake. For all he knows, there might not even be a Sea-in-the-Sky.

The Steward sets down her bag not far from the window, unfastens it, and begins rummaging. She pulls out a fishing net for the door, accidentally grabbing one of her shell-covered mirrors along with it. She stuffs the mirror back in the bag, but not before Gauge gets a glimpse of the glass.

"Did you see that?" he asks.

"See what?" Roux whispers.

"The mirror."

"No, why?"

"The glass is cracked."

"So what?"

Gauge pulls the pieces of mirror he took from the Wharves out of his pocket. The halves are cracked in an unnaturally straight line, exactly like the line on the mirror he just saw.

(I'm so excited that the boy is finally paying attention to my clue that I drop my front legs to the ground and wiggle my rear. The undignified display of canine enthusiasm makes me grateful that I'm invisible.)

"That's it!" Gauge tucks the mirror pieces back in his pocket. "If we can prove she uses pre-cracked mirrors, we can convince everyone that they are being deceived, that the Release is fake. The Wolf knows this—that's why she tried to steal my mirror."

"The Wolf tried to *what?*"

Gauge cringes. "I didn't want to scare you. But when I woke up earlier, the Wolf was by my bed."

Roux folds her arms. "You didn't want to scare me?"

"I didn't know how you'd feel about the Wolf being in your living room. But if I'm right, we can use these mirrors to get to the Wolf."

Roux shakes her head. "Are you out to sea? How are we going to get our hands on the Steward's mirrors?"

"We have to check her supply. Find out if they are all broken."

"You're going to break into her house?"

"Not break in. Visit."

"You *are* out to sea. Without a paddle."

A gull squawks overhead as if agreeing with Roux.

"You don't have to come if you don't want to, but I'm going to find out."

"Do you know what will happen if you're caught?"

"Let me think." Gauge puts his fingers on his chin. "They'll put up posters of me all over the village with a bounty on my head? No, wait a minute. They'll set me out to sea."

"This isn't a joke," Roux says.

"I'm doing this whether you help me or not."

"Fine," Roux says. "But let's do it quickly, while the Steward is busy."

Minutes later, they approach the Steward's home with a rough plan in place. Roux wipes her hands on her skirt. "You sure about this?"

"No," Gauge says flatly. "But I'm doing it anyway."

He tucks himself behind a barrel while Roux knocks. Abeline the Keeper answers the door, peering over her pointed nose, her sky-blue eyes full of suspicion. Roux explains that she needs to speak with the Steward and accepts the Keeper's invitation to wait in the sitting room for the Steward's return. (Roux plans to act distraught over the fact that she didn't bring a lantern to her father's Release. She's resourceful, I'll give her that.)

While the Keeper shows Roux the way, Gauge

slips through the front door. He gapes at the home's opulence. Heavy rugs line the floors. Rich paintings fill the walls. Ornate pottery and elaborate sculptures rest on displays throughout the main level. The boy thought the Vessel-maker lived in luxury, but his living room seems dull by comparison.

This is no time to stand about gawking. He decides to start his search in the cellar, reasoning that's where the Steward would be most likely to hide items she wants to keep secret. He tiptoes down the stairs, cringing as one of them groans.

At the bottom, he finds a small room with jagged rock walls lined with stocked shelves. His eyes adjust to the dark. The little bit of light sneaking in from upstairs reveals that the shelves hold only hard cheeses, potatoes, and dried fish—pantry items.

He hoped to avoid searching the main level, but there's no choice. He's on the third step when he hears the front door open. The Steward's voice floats down to him. The boy freezes. He can either sneak upstairs as soon as her voice fades and hope to escape undetected or he can hide in the pantry and wait for the dark of night to continue his search.

He inches back downstairs and squeezes himself behind a barrel of what is either herring or pickles. The space is dark and cramped, and time passes slowly. (Roux has long since finished her conversation with the Steward and, not knowing what else to do, returned home, where she anxiously awaits Gauge's arrival.) Exhaustion tugs at the boy, but his nerves won't let him relax. Even if he's not discovered, he can't escape the feeling that I'm lurking about, that I might make an appearance at any moment.

Indeed, this would be the perfect opportunity to confront the boy. If he still refused to talk, or worse, refused to accept my job, I could easily create enough chaos to draw the attention of everyone in the house, guaranteeing the boy's arrest.

He'd almost certainly be sentenced to be put out to sea, leaving him with no choice but to accept my offer. The timing would be none too soon; no matter how I groom, the stench of rotten moss seems to permeate my coat. It's as if the Bog has already started to claim me.

Unfortunately, there's been a terrible shipwreck not far offshore, and even though the sailors aren't from

Gatineau, they are within my territory and therefore my responsibility. I hurry, but my task isn't an easy one, and I'm afraid I won't finish before the boy takes his leave.

The stairs creak, warning the boy that he's about to get a visitor. The door opens and flickering light floods the room. Gauge holds his breath, desperate to peek but not daring to move. Footsteps shuffle around the cellar. Two jars clank together. If whoever is in the room comes for whatever is in the barrel he's hiding behind, the boy is doomed. He squeezes his eyes shut. Finally, the door creaks and then latches, leaving the boy in silence.

He lets out a sigh of relief. That was close. But the interruption gave him a good sense of the time—it was almost certainly the cook working on preparations for tomorrow's breakfast. He guesses it will be only another hour before the house is quiet.

The boy's muscles cramp and burn. He rolls his neck and attempts to shift his weight. It doesn't work. He raises himself slowly, ready to dive back down at the slightest hint of another visitor. When none arrive, he gradually relaxes. After what he hopes is an hour, he opens the door slowly, listening for any signs of activity. (I'm not even close to finished with my task. I've never been a particularly accomplished swimmer, and finding bodies on the sea floor is one of my more difficult responsibilities.)

The house is silent. Gauge creeps upward, hoping to avoid the creaky stair but finding it all the same. He straightens up on the main level, letting his eyes adjust to the moonlight shining in through the windows. The front door is straight ahead. He should make a break for it, escape while he can. But the study where Roux waited calls to him. What if the Steward's mirrors are there?

His curiosity wins out and he tiptoes inside. Two of his grandpapá's chairs share a square table that features a small statue of a naked woman whose bottom half is a goat. A faun. His grandpapá told him stories of such creatures. He stares at it, fascinated.

In the room above his head, someone lets out a loud snore. It must be the Steward, but he's surprised women snore. (Impertinent, if you ask me. Not that I have to worry about such matters—sleep was one of the many things I gave up when I accepted my position.)

The Steward tosses and turns. A particularly loud snore snaps Gauge out of his thinking spell and he continues across the room to a delicate desk in the corner. Beside it, a majestic hutch with closed doors steals the boy's attention. He runs a hand along the smooth wood. Cherry isn't easy to come by. The boy has a small fox carved from the red-tinged wood, but he can't think of the last time his grandpapá had anything cherry in the shop. He holds his breath as he unfastens the latch and eases the doors open.

Dozens of shelled mirrors are stacked in front of him. Gauge holds one up to the window. It glints in the moonlight. Just as he suspected. A crack runs down the middle of the glass. He inspects another. And another. They are all cracked exactly in half in the same straight line.

Frowning, he stacks them carefully back in the cabinet. As he's shutting the door, he spots a chisel and small hammer resting on the bottom shelf. He holds the chisel against a mirror, confirming that it's the right size to make the cracks. Behind him, someone gasps. A candlelit figure fills the doorway.

"What in the sea—" the Steward gasps.

Gauge drops the chisel but clutches the mirror as he dashes across the room, intending to dive under her legs. On edge from what is now four deaths in five days (a number she's conveniently forgetting is only ever so slightly higher than usual), she misunderstands his intentions and lunges out of reach, shrieking, "The Voyant! Help!"

The boy lets himself out the front door and sprints down the street, daring only a quick look back—enough to see the Steward and the Keeper on the front stoop, yelling for help.

He stuffs the mirror in his pocket but doesn't slow until he's safely back inside the smithy.

Roux rises from the table. "Thank the Seven Seas," she says, clasping a hand to her chest. "Where have you been? What happened?"

Gauge explains how he was trapped in the cellar and only barely managed to escape.

"Do you think they recognized you?"

"I know for sure they did," Gauge says, rubbing his head.

Roux paces the room, pulling her hair. "This is bad. This is very bad. They're going to double down on finding you, you know."

"I know," Gauge says. "But it was worth it."

He pulls out the Steward's mirror and the broken mirror from his grandpapá's Release—*fake Release,* he thinks, making a face—and places them on the table in front of him. "They're all pre-cracked."

Roux inspects the mirrors and then looks up at Gauge. "We have to figure out how to expose Lord Mayor Vulpine—and force him to help us find the Wolf—before they find you."

"Exactly," Gauge says. "And I think I know how."

Chapter Thirteen

"You can't expect us to break into the Paper-maker's shop—we're already in enough trouble!" Roux exclaims after hearing Gauge's plan.

"We don't have to," he says. "We can use the posters that are already out."

They agree to split up and race through the village collecting as many sheets as they can. At one point, Gauge rounds a corner and nearly comes face-to-face with a Guard making his rounds. Luckily, the Guard is distracted by a mewling kitten, giving the boy time to retreat.

They work through what's left of the night, writing a simple note on the back of each sheet: "TRAITOR REVEALED (High Noon at the Square)."

As Roux finishes the last notice, Gauge pokes at the dying fire, spreading the ashes to diffuse their heat. He wishes he could add another log and curl up in bed, but they can't stop now. Roux pulls a shawl over her shoulders and they hurry outside, where they're greeted by the sun's first rays.

The boy's heart beats frantically in his chest. There will be no turning back—not after this. They make it to the neighbor's door before stopping abruptly. A new poster hangs there, featuring an exact likeness of Gauge's face. This time, they got everything right— the mouth, the eyes, the chin—even his new haircut.

He throws his head back and shuts his eyes. "For the love of all the sharks in the sea," he groans.

"You're going to have to wait at the shop," Roux says. "I can put all these up without attracting notice."

The boy lets himself back into the shop but then lifts a shade, watching until Roux disappears. A knot forms in his stomach. "Smooth sailing," he whispers.

The smart thing to do would be to sleep, to pre- pare for what's to come, but the boy won't let him- self rest—not when Roux is out on the streets doing the work he should be helping with. A fresh round of worry grips him. If their plan doesn't work, if the ship sails without him . . . He longs for his folding knife, for a piece of wood to focus on. He sinks down at the grindstone, pulls the metal heart from his pocket, and begins working.

After the better part of an hour, he stops. He inspects his work, admiring the smooth edges and shiny metal. *I don't believe the Blacksmith could have done any better*, he tells himself. He'll give it to Roux the moment she returns. He imagines her clutching it to her chest, happiness streaming from her eyes.

Pounding sounds from the front door.

"Let us in!" harsh voices shout.

Gauge races for the back, slipping the heart in his pocket as he runs. But the moment he enters the living room, he's forced to stop. Three armed Guards stand inside, blocking the door. They carry torches to protect themselves from the Wolf. The flames flicker an ominous warning.

"There he is!" one of the Guards shouts, pointing at Gauge.

It's the nasty Guard from the Wharves. Gauge's knees weaken, but he forces himself to remain on his feet.

Another Guard—the one in charge, judging from his cocky swagger and the red sash tied at his waist—steps forward, peering into Gauge's face with algae-colored eyes that stand out against his tanned skin. "That's him, all right."

"How did you find me?" Gauge asks.

"Thought I recognized you back at the Wharves," the nasty one says. "But Snatty convinced me I was one fish short of a haul."

Gauge figures Snatty must be the Guard who helped bury his grandpapá.

"When I saw your poster this morning, I knew it was you."

"How did you know I was here?"

"Wife mentioned she saw Woolsey the Blacksmith's daughter at the market with a new Apprentice. Knew the Blacksmith was released—no need for a new Apprentice."

Gauge curses himself. Roux was right—he shouldn't have been running all over the village.

Roux. Gauge utters a silent plea that she won't pick right now to make an appearance. "The Blacksmith's daughter has nothing to do with anything. I didn't tell her who I was."

"Lord Mayor Vulpine will be the judge of that," the head Guard says. He hands his torch to another Guard and binds Gauge's hands in front of him.

Gauge winces as the rope digs into his skin.

"This is hardly the worst of your problems," the Guard says. "Now let's go. And no trickery with the Wolf or it's—"

The Guard slices a finger across his own neck.

As they walk through the village, a crowd builds behind them. "Stinking Voyant," someone calls. An egg cracks on the back of Gauge's head, spilling its slimy contents down his neck and under his collar.

"Set him out to sea!" someone else calls.

Chants of "Set him out to sea" follow the boy all the way to the square. A giant fire roars in the center, lit to fend me off should the boy summon me.

Gauge is forced to stand on the platform at the front of the crowd. The taunting continues, but the insults roll off his skin like water on the grindstone. Some people are here to witness a Voyant's trial, but the posters Roux put out undoubtedly have others convinced that there's more to the story. Gauge trembles with anticipation. This is it—his chance to reveal Lord Mayor Vulpine's treachery, to set the record straight.

Lord Mayor Vulpine mounts the platform and stands behind his podium. He shoots a fleeting glance toward Gauge and grimaces like he's swallowed a spoiled oyster. "Where's the girl?" he asks a Guard.

"Still looking," the Guard says.

"Bring her here when you find her."

"No!" Gauge cries. "She has nothing to do with this. Let her be!"

Lord Mayor Vulpine ignores Gauge's outburst. "Make haste," he tells his Guard.

Gauge shakes. Maybe they won't find her until this is all over.

He feels the heart hanging in his pocket, hears the Blacksmith's words. *Promise me you'll take care of things.*

Gauge swallows, his throat suddenly dry and scratchy.

Lord Mayor Vulpine calls for the growing crowd to settle. "By the power vested in me by Grand Lord Lasage, I declare this trial begun," he says. "In it, I shall serve as jury and judge and my sentence shall be binding. Are there any objections?"

Silence fills the air. The boy has strong objections, but Lord Mayor Vulpine's words wrap around him like tentacles, squeezing the air from his chest. His chin drops. He can't gather his breath, can't force words from his mouth.

"I hereby charge Gauge the Apprentice, grandson of the late Carpenter, as a Voyant. In addition, I will bring forth evidence showing he broke into the house of our esteemed Steward, Mistress Charbonneaux."

A collective gasp rises from the crowd. They were expecting a Voyant. But a thief?

Gauge knows this is his chance to speak up, but his tongue is anchored at the bottom of his mouth, thick and heavy.

"What proof can you provide?" someone yells.

"I told you at our last assembly that the boy already caused at least one death. The truth is, several winters ago he caused my beloved wife to set sail." Lord Mayor Vulpine's words catch in his throat. He makes a great show of taking out a silky kerchief and dotting the corners of his eyes. (This is not to say his grief isn't genuine. Only that he's not above playing it to his advantage.)

The crowd murmurs. They have heard rumors, but Lord Mayor Vulpine never publicly addressed the death of Mistress Vulpine.

"Why wasn't he put on trial?" another voice yells.

Lord Mayor Vulpine adjusts his collar. He doesn't want to admit he ordered the boy to be set out to sea without a trial. "When I sent my Guard to retrieve the boy, he came back empty-handed. Claimed the boy attempted to call the Wolf, and he was forced to act in self-defense."

Rage bubbles up in Gauge, loosening his tongue. "None of this is true," he yells.

Lord Mayor Vulpine's eyes blaze with barely contained fury.

The boy feels the heat of an entire village staring at him. He remembers the Blacksmith's plea. He has to speak up. For himself. For Roux. "I won't bother denying that I'm a Voyant. But I'm not from the Bog, and I've never done anything to hurt any of you. The truth is, I don't know *why* I can see the Wolf. But I hate her as much as you do."

"Her?" someone yells.

"Yes, her." The boy draws a deep breath, tries to order his thoughts, to focus on what's important. "Lord Mayor Vulpine has filled your head with lies. About death, about our Release ceremonies. He's a Voyant himself. Only he made a deal with the Wolf. He and the Steward and—"

Lord Mayor Vulpine steps in. "I think we've heard quite enough."

"I'm not done," Gauge yells.

The crowd roars.

"Let him speak." An authoritative voice fills the air.

Gauge searches for the source. The kind Guard from the Wharves. Snatty.

"If there is a conspiracy, I, for one, would like to hear it."

"But there's no—the boy is—" Lord Mayor Vulpine sputters, his face glowing red.

"Let him speak!" someone else yells. The rest of the crowd joins in.

Hope swells in Gauge's chest. If he can get them to listen, to see the truth, then maybe, just maybe . . .

"Very well," Lord Mayor Vulpine says. "But I

assure you, the boy speaks utter nonsense." (You may be surprised at how easily he gives in, but he's entirely thrown off by the confrontation. Most bullies are cowards at heart.)

Gauge gathers his courage and continues. "Since my grandpapá set sail, I've been tracking the Wolf. Over the last few days, I've discovered that the Release isn't what we believe it to be."

"What do you mean?" someone yells.

"The oars, the lantern, the shaving—none of it matters. None of it helps those who have set sail."

Gauge pauses, waiting for the crowd to absorb the truth of his words.

"Boy, don't you think we know that?" An elderly woman pushes her way through the crowd, coming to rest with her wrinkled hand on a cane embellished with sea turtles carved by Gauge's grandpapá.

His stomach flops like a half-dead fish. They all *know* none of that stuff is necessary? That can't be. They must not understand. He maneuvers his tied-together wrists to pull the halves of the seashell-crusted mirror from his pocket. "The mirrors, they don't release our souls from our bodies. They're pre-broken. Look how straight and perfect the lines are."

Someone yells, "Do you have evidence that Lord Mayor Vulpine is working with the Wolf or not?"

"Check the Steward's study," Gauge says, sweat beading on his brow. "You'll find her tools there. The Steward, the Lord Mayor, they do all these things to fool you. The Wolf steals our souls before they get to any of this. I saw Lord Mayor Vulpine pay off the Healer for her silence this very afternoon."

Lord Mayor Vulpine shouts, "That was payment for my heart medicine, you imbecile!"

The Guards grab Gauge's elbows. He drops the pieces of mirror. The glass smashes, spreading shards around his feet.

Gauge searches out Snatty's face, seeking some confirmation that he believes what Gauge is saying. Snatty shakes his head, pity shining from his eyes. Gauge thinks about all of the gifts Roux's neighbors brought to the smithy—food, fishing gear—items they could ill-afford to spare. "What about the vessels—why go into debt for things that don't even help?"

The Steward straightens her shoulders. She doesn't

know what to make of the boy's story. She's terrified he might call the Wolf, but she's proud of the work she does, work it's important the boy understand. "Not everything has to be real to be true," she says. "We do these things to help manage our grief, to pay our respects to those who set sail."

"I'll not see my family off in anything less than the best," someone calls. "I don't care what it costs me."

Gauge is stunned. All the rituals—the entire Release—it really is a scam, only the whole village knows about it. "You're liars," he yells, a river of hot tears streaming down his face. "All of you lie."

His accusation sends ripples of shock through the crowd.

Gauge continues shouting. "What about my grand-papá? You made me release him all on my own. He was a good man. He deserved more. Not one of you paid your respects. Not one of you cared that he was gone. Not one of you thought about how I might feel, the help I might need. You're all so busy being scared that you closed us off, pretended we didn't exist. We needed you—he needed you. *I* needed you."

He breaks down.

The faces in the crowd are no longer fearful. Some bow their heads, ashamed. Others study Gauge with sad eyes. Somehow, this is worse than their fear. Worse than being invisible.

"We never meant to deceive you," the Steward says gently.

(That being the case, you are undoubtedly wondering why the Steward goes through the trouble of pre-breaking the mirrors. Although the break is symbolic, it distresses survivors to see a mirror splinter or shatter over their loved ones.)

The Steward goes on. "We don't know if anything we do helps the departed reach the Sea-in-the-Sky. But the ritual is part of letting go. Sometimes, these things are hard to talk about with children, but your grandpapá, he should have helped you understand."

Gauge remembers his strange conversation with the Healer after the Blacksmith set sail. She'd been trying to tell him, to prepare him for this moment. He raises his head. "So there is a Sea-in-the-Sky?"

The Steward looks perplexed. "Of course there is. You've seen the lanterns yourself."

(The villagers would never think to question the

existence of the Sea-in-the-Sky. As far as they're concerned, it's a fact, much like the Earth is round, the
sky green. Yes, I know it's blue. I was checking to
make sure you're paying attention.)

Gauge spots a boy a few winters younger than him
clinging to his mother, tears rolling down his cheeks.
A much younger girl sobs into her father's shoulder.
They didn't know the truth, either.

Again his anger bubbles up, this time directed at
his grandpapá. The old man should have told him,
should have prepared him for the world. Instead, he
threw Gauge in the deep sea and left him to drown.

Lord Mayor Vulpine clears his throat. "We must
return to the matter at hand. The boy is, by his own
admission, a Voyant."

Someone yells from the crowd, "He seems harmless to me."

Another voice yells, "Maybe he can help us track
the Wolf."

The crowd murmurs in agreement.

For several winters, Lord Mayor Vulpine blamed
Gauge for the loss of his wife. Seeing the snot-nosed
kid in front of him, hearing his confusion, the man is

no longer so sure. But even if the boy didn't cause the death of Mistress Vulpine, he has no doubt the boy is tied to me, and nothing good can come of that.

In any case, Lord Mayor Vulpine isn't willing to dig too deeply into all this. Not when doing so would require him to think about what really happened the night his wife set sail. Besides, he can't appear weak.

He straightens. "As tempting as the boy's offer to track the Wolf is, we can't know if he's telling the truth. It may be that he's only trying to save his own sloop, lure us into some kind of trap."

The crowd considers Lord Mayor Vulpine's words.

He continues. "He entered the Steward's house in the dark of night. We cannot be safe if there is even one among us willing to break the law. On this point, the consequences are clear. The boy *must* be set out to sea."

Lord Mayor Vulpine raises his chin, puffs his chest, dares anyone to contradict him. The crowd shifts, eyeing first the boy and then Lord Mayor Vulpine. There's no denying that what he said is true—rules have to be upheld for the safety of the entire village.

But this isn't like catching a fish, where there is either one at the end of your line or not. This is more like teetering on the edge of a boat with a great white shark nearby.

Gauge faces the crowd, trying to make eye contact with someone, anyone, who might speak up for him. Snatty's eyes are down, though his expression is pained. The Steward also avoids looking at the boy. She fixes her gaze on a caterpillar crawling on the ground, on its futile search for an escape from the crowd.

There's a part of her that believes what the boy is saying—that he's innocent, that he might help rid the village of the Wolf. But her fear is woven into her soul, a constant since the day she was born. (Of course, there's also the little matter of her own ambition. She's been working to recruit allies but hasn't yet amassed enough power to risk a confrontation with Lord Mayor Vulpine.)

Everything around Gauge fades as the podium catches his attention. He always had the impression it was a grand thing, but the wood is warped and rotting. *Grandpapá could fix that right up.*

Gauge hangs his head. A scuff mars the tip of his boot.

(Seeing the dejection on Gauge's face, my heart goes out to the boy. Truly. But I take comfort in knowing that this will be behind him soon. Now he'll have to accept my offer.)

Lord Mayor Vulpine turns to his Guards. "Take him away."

Chapter Fourteen

Gauge doesn't bother fighting for his freedom. He's escorted to Lord Mayor Vulpine's home, where he'll be kept for a single night in order to write out his final goodbyes. (As if the boy is leaving behind any family who might care.)

On the second floor, his wrists are unbound and he's thrown in a large, mostly empty room. A simple writing desk holding ink, quills, and a handful of corked bottles waits in the corner.

The door shuts behind Gauge. Two locks click. He rushes to the open window. The sea crashes into the cliffs far below. A ship sails toward the horizon and eventually disappears, taking with it his only real chance of survival.

The boy paces the room. His own death is certain, but he can't stop thinking about Roux. If only he'd never gotten her involved. He smiles sadly, remembering her fierce determination to help him, her quick wit, the way she tugs on her hair when she's nervous or upset. She already lost her mother and her father—now she's going to lose a friend, too.

Gauge feels his cheeks flame. Does she think of him as a friend? He remembers the warmth in her eyes. She's the one person who accepts him for who he is, who doesn't blame him for a connection with a Wolf that he doesn't want and can't control.

He cringes, thinking of Lord Mayor Vulpine's Guards finding her and binding her wrists.

Maybe she'll escape. Find someplace to hide until all this has passed.

Or maybe Lord Mayor Vulpine will decide Gauge's punishment is enough and let her go free. Knowing she's safe—or even that she might be—gives the boy the courage to face what's to come. He knows there's no hope for him. Not this time. He squares his shoulders. The crowd will expect him to cry and wail, to beg for mercy as he's being set out to sea. He won't give them the satisfaction. Grandpapá wouldn't want him to give up his pride, his dignity.

Hours later, the locks click and the door opens. Roux stumbles inside and falls to her knees. She doesn't speak, only curls into a ball and rocks back and forth, pulling at her hair.

Gauge crouches at her side. "Are you injured? Did they hurt you?"

"This can't be happening," she moans. "Not again."

Gauge remembers the woman he saw at the square with his grandpapá when he was little. Roux's fierce determination to stop Lord Mayor Vulpine. "Your mother, was she . . . ?"

"She was accused of witchery, same as you," Roux sobs.

"Was she a Voyant?" Gauge asks.

Roux lifts her head, revealing a tear-streaked face. "Her only crime was speaking out against Lord Mayor Vulpine's taxes."

"We'll find some way out of here," Gauge promises, suddenly desperate to make the impossible happen. "We have to."

She doesn't seem to hear him. The boy resumes

pacing. They'd never survive an escape out the window. He inspects the solid oak door, wishing he had a crowbar to pry it open. "How many Guards are posted outside?"

Roux sniffles. "Two."

"Maybe we can overpower them the next time the door opens," Gauge says hopefully.

"Sure. We'll overpower two armed Guards and escape into a house, a village, all eager for our deaths. Good plan."

"We'll go straight to the docks. Borrow a boat. Start a new life somewhere else."

"Do you really think they're going to let us sail off into the sunset? That they wouldn't come after us? Gauge, give it up. We're done for."

He folds onto the floor next to her. "I'm sorry," he says. "I never meant for any of this to happen."

"I know." She rises to her knees and wipes away her tears, then forces herself to meet his gaze.

He sees sadness and despair but also tenderness. He aches for all that they will miss, for the friendship they might have enjoyed, for whatever that might have become. He slips his hand in his pocket and pulls out the small metal heart. He turns it over in his hands and then presses it into hers. "This is for you."

She grips it tightly. "Is it from—"

"Your father started it," Gauge says. "He wanted you to have it."

"Gauge, it's . . ." She presses the heart to her chest. Her eyes shine with gratitude and appreciation, with happiness and sadness mixed together like grains of sand swirling in a wave. "It's perfect."

The boy bows his head. She deserves so much more than this.

The heart sparks a flame of hope in Roux.

"There must be a way out of this mess." She rises and approaches the window. "Maybe tomorrow. They have to walk us to the beach—we can escape then. Or maybe we can jump out of the boat and swim to shore?"

Gauge joins her but doesn't answer. He doesn't want to dash her hope.

"It could work," she says. "We have to try. Gauge, why aren't you saying anything?"

"I can't swim," he finally says.

Beneath them, hungry waves beat against the cliffs.

. . .

When they turn around, I'm sitting in front of them, my head cocked.

The boy's eyes flash with anger and then confusion. "What are you doing here?"

"What is it?" Roux asks, inching closer to him. "Is it the Wolf?"

Gauge doesn't answer.

"I've come to help."

"Help how?" Gauge asks. "You're the reason I'm being set out to sea in the first place."

"An unfortunate side effect of your gift."

"My *gift*?"

"Haven't you ever wondered why you're the only one who can see me?"

"A million times. But that's not a *gift*, it's a *curse*."

"What would you say if I offered you a chance to save both of your lives?"

"I'd say yes." Gauge narrows his eyes. "Wait a minute. Is this about the job you mentioned?"

"Job?" Roux asks.

I lick my lips. "I'm old and my bones are achy—I need rest. Take my place and you'll be able to walk right past the Guards."

Distrust flickers in the boy's eyes, along with the tiniest flame of hope. "What about Roux?"

"What *about* me?" Roux asks.

Gauge holds up a finger.

"Simple." My next words nearly stick in my throat, but I force them out. "I'll save her."

The relief in the boy's eyes is quickly replaced by suspicion. He crosses his arms. "What do you do with them?"

"Pardon?"

"I thought you fed the souls to your pups, but that's not a *job*."

"I don't feed the souls to anyone. I deliver them to Mother Wolf's den."

Gauge backs away, pulling Roux with him. "So you do steal them."

"I don't steal anything." I fight to keep the exasperation out of my voice. "I'm a Courier."

He eyes me warily. "What does your *Mother Wolf* do with them?"

"Mother Wolf?" Roux cries. "Gauge, what's going on?"

"I'm not sure yet."

"She cares for them until they are strong enough to survive in the Woods Beyond."

The boy's forehead wrinkles. "The Woods Beyond?"

"Where we go when we finish here."

"What about the Sea-in-the-Sky?"

I shake my head.

Gauge rubs the back of his neck. "How do I know you aren't working with the Steward or Nicoline the Healer? Or Lord Mayor Vulpine?"

"How could I be working with them when you're the only person who can see or hear me?"

"So Lord Mayor Vulpine isn't a Voyant?"

"Definitely not."

"Why should I believe anything you say?"

I scratch behind my ear. "What other choice do you have?"

Silence stretches between us.

Finally, Gauge speaks. "What about my grand-papá? Is he safe?"

I answer the question as best I can. "The Woods Beyond, they're a resting place, a better place, for all of us."

Gauge shakes, trying to absorb the news that his grandpapá is unharmed. That I didn't steal the old man to feed to my pups. That I'm not what he thought—that nothing is. "If I agree, will I be able to see him?"

This question knocks the wind from my lungs. It's nearly the same one I asked the former Wolf so very long ago. I would have done anything—agreed to anything—for one more chance to see my daughter, to hold her in my arms.

The words burn as they come out. "You will."

Gauge's knees give out. If he accepts the job, he'll get to save Roux *and* see his grandpapá. He sinks to the floor.

"Gauge, are you all right?" Roux asks.

The boy sees the welts around her wrists from the ropes, imagines her floating out at sea. He can't tell me no, can't be responsible for her death.

"I need an answer," I say.

He sucks in a deep breath and prepares to accept my offer. I rise to my feet, panting.

"Your grandpapá warned you about the Wolf," Roux reminds him.

Gauge's head tilts. Doubt fills his eyes.

No. *No, no, no, no, no.*

"How did my grandpapá know you were still around at the end?" he asks.

"I knew your mother," I say, hoping to regain his trust. (This news can't possibly come as a surprise to you. Why else would the old man have warned the boy about me if he didn't know who I was, what I wanted?)

My arrow hits its mark.

"What? How?"

"She was a Voyant, like you. She would have taken this job if sickness hadn't claimed her." (This is a stretch—she was clear that she'd never leave her son. Still, with more time, I might have been able to change her mind.)

The boy shakes his head. "No, I don't believe you. My mother, she loved me. Grandpapá said I was her everything."

I hate the pain in the boy's eyes, but I can't let this chance slip away. "She understood how important this job is."

"Important how? Can't this *Mother Wolf* of yours

find someone else to do her dirty work?"

"It's not dirty work," I growl, surprised by how his accusation stings. "What I do is important. If I don't deliver the souls, they'll remain stuck in the body. Eventually, they'll rot and sink down to the Bog."

The boy's chin trembles. "Find someone else."

"There is no one else. You're only the third Voyant in seven hundred winters. And I'm not getting any younger. Your mother knew all of this. She knew that this job was an honor, a duty for those who have the gift." All this is true. I've done the job to the best of my ability, treated each soul with the tender care it deserves.

But I've shouldered the burden far longer than anyone should have to bear. I can't stop thinking about the centuries of loneliness. The hatred of the villagers. I thought becoming the Wolf would be a gift, a chance to reconnect with my daughter. Instead, my life turned into a never-ending curse.

I can't meet the boy's eyes.

Gauge jumps to his feet. "What aren't you telling me?"

I don't answer.

A tickle appears in the back of the boy's mind, something that doesn't quite make sense. He thinks out loud. "You're lying. This is a trick."

"No," I cry. "You have to accept."

"You don't care what happens to me," Gauge says. "And you can't help Roux. You're only looking out for yourself."

I whimper.

Gauge steps back and takes Roux's hand. "I want you to leave. Now."

Centuries of anger and resentment brew inside me, a toxic mix of rage that spews from my mouth. I've done my job, and done it the best I can. But I'm tired. So tired. I can't do it anymore. I *won't* do it anymore.

I bare my teeth and snarl. Roux can't see or hear me, but she senses something is wrong and recoils.

The boy grips her hand, determined to offer what little comfort he can.

I hate myself for what I'm about to do, but it has to be done. I step closer. "Accept the job willingly, or I'll force it on you."

"No," Gauge says softly.

I emit a low, threatening growl.

"Go ahead," Gauge says. "Kill me."

He steps closer. Close enough that I could reach out, snatch his neck in my mouth, and give him one hard shake. Call death.

Except I can't.

And he knows it.

Chapter Fifteen

I'd like to say that I accept my defeat gracefully. That I walk away with my head high, my dignity intact. Nothing could be further from the truth.

The moment I realize he's truly rejecting my offer, I crumble. I whine, I shake, and I wail. "No," I howl. "Nooooooooooo!"

As I grieve, I'm faced with a single, inescapable fact: I failed. Not only myself, but my daughter. I won't be joining Émilie anytime soon. I may never be able to join her. The weight of my grief crushes my chest, sucks the air from my lungs.

I was close. So close that I was able to taste it. To smell it (success smells of eggs and sugar—like a custard but stronger and laced with ripe berries). How many times I imagined our reunion—the weight of her jumping into my arms, the soft touch of her chubby hands on my face as she showered me with sloppy kisses.

Now that I started down this path, memories I fought hundreds of winters to forget flood my mind. I remember the moment she was first placed in my arms—the moment her dark, stormy eyes peered up at me, softening in recognition. The moment I first touched her smooth cheek, the moment I stroked her silken hair.

I remember the moment she discovered she could roll around on the floor. The moment she finally started crawling and then, later, when she let go of the hearth and took her first, tentative steps into my open arms. She trusted that I would be there to catch her before she wobbled and fell.

"I'll always catch you," I whispered.

But I didn't. I was busy beating the wash when she toddled away, when she set out to explore the world. By the time I noticed, she'd already made it some distance off, already neared the well.

"Stop! Émilie, stop!" I screamed.

But she didn't stop. She teetered on, determined to prove her independence.

The world came to a standstill as I dropped my laundry. Sprinted toward her.

Arrived too late.

She was silent as she fell, a single splash her only farewell.

I was numb when the Wolf appeared—the same Wolf that had stalked me my whole life. How quickly the dark void in my chest changed to excitement and gratitude when the Wolf finally approached me, when he offered up a chance to see Émilie again.

I accepted without hesitation, not knowing the truth—that I'd been tricked. That as the Wolf, I couldn't see my baby. Wouldn't see her until I found a Voyant to take my spot, until I journeyed to the Woods Beyond to join her.

My body trembles as it struggles to contain the grief I spent centuries holding in.

While I curl into a tight ball and bury my face under my paws, the boy's hand slides to grip the hilt of his knife. The Guards didn't bother to check him for weapons. They didn't dream that a boy would think to carry one.

This is the opportunity he's been waiting for. How easy it would be to pull the knife out now, to attack. It's no less than I deserve—even if I didn't steal his grandpapá or the Blacksmith, or anyone else, I tried to trick him. I lied.

He sees that my guard is down, imagines making one clean cut across my neck. But he hesitates. He's filled with anger—at the villagers, for refusing to stand by him and his grandpapá, for sentencing him to a death he doesn't deserve, for sentencing Roux to a death she most definitely doesn't deserve. At me—for everything.

But he's angry at himself, too. Had he really thought that his grandpapá's soul would row up to the Sea-in-the-Sky? How could he, in a vessel that had already been buried? The villagers, they hadn't deceived him intentionally. He was too busy seeking revenge, too busy proving he was right, to see the truth. Killing me won't solve anything.

The boy's hand falls to his side. Truthfully, it was easier to focus on his anger, to blame me, than it was to face the inescapable truth: that his grandpapá is dead. Gone. That he's never coming back. That Gauge is alone.

He'll never again hear the old man's gravelly voice explain which vegetables are ready for picking. His grandpapá won't be there to keep him safe, to guide him through whatever challenges come his way. He won't be there to see Gauge grow, to see him greet his first customer. Become a Master Carpenter. One day get married, become a father.

The boy falls to his knees. He won't take my job, not when it would mean abandoning Roux. They'll both be set out to sea in a matter of hours. He can cling to his anger, continue using it as a shield to keep himself from feeling more than he has to in the little time he has left. Or he can choose to live out his last moments filled with the grace that he begged the villagers to show him. He knows what it is to be desperate, to be rejected.

Slowly, tentatively, he reaches out his hand. It settles on my back, warm and steady.

Roux moves to the boy's side. The long lashes rimming her large eyes remind me of my daughter. Is this what Émilie would have looked like if she'd survived?

"What's your name?" Roux asks.

Again, the breath is sucked from my chest. It's been over seven hundred winters since anyone has known—or cared— about my name.

Gauge isn't sure if I can hear anyone but him. "Do you have a name?" he asks.

"Alouette," I whisper. "I used to be called Alouette." Gauge repeats it to Roux.

She reaches out, feels the air. Gauge guides her hand to my snout. I sniff. She smells of bright tulips on a spring day. Of freshly baked bread. Of a mother licking her newborn pup. She smells like Émilie.

I picture my daughter running toward the well, remember watching helplessly as she tumbled over the side.

Now two more lives are going to be cut short because of me. I can't let that happen.

I rise and shake out my fur. "I'm going to get you out of here."

"What's the use, if we're all going to end up in the Bog anyway?" Gauge asks.

I'm still old and tired, but the grace these two

have shown has touched my heart, breathed life into my body and spirit. I'll continue fetching souls and delivering them to Mother Wolf's den until another Voyant comes along. "That's not going to happen."

Hope lights the boy's eyes. "Can you magic us out?"

"I'm afraid not. But there must be another way."

The boy's chin quivers as a lonely gull cries in the distance.

I pace the room, searching for a solution. Seconds or minutes or hours later, I whirl toward Gauge. "I need you to write a note."

"What kind of note?"

"A simple one. Tell the truth about you and me. Like you did at the square."

"To whom?"

"Let me worry about that."

In my seven hundred winters I picked up a few talents. Like how to read people. And I think I know exactly who to turn to for help.

The boy studies me, tries to decide if I'm trustworthy. He makes his way to the desk. "I hope you know what you're doing."

He hunches over the paper, biting his bottom lip

and squinting as he writes, using what little light is left from the already setting sun. Roux hovers behind him, critiquing his penmanship and grammar, only falling silent when Gauge asks if she'd like to do it herself. (As a former scribe, I'm actually quite impressed with the boy's handwriting.)

I leave the room with the bottled note clenched in my mouth and find Nicoline the Healer tucked in bed, unable to sleep. She was with a patient the previous night and through most of the day, so she didn't witness the events at the square personally, but she heard what transpired soon after. She's not at all happy but feels powerless to do anything. Finally, she realizes sleep will be a long time in coming, lights a candle, and reaches for the soft leather journal by her bed.

Noticing the bottle I placed there, she startles before snatching it up and freeing the paper inside.

To Whoever Reads This Note,

I won't bother denying that I can see the Wolf.
But I'm not from the Bog and I don't control

her. Neither the Wolf nor I have ever hurt
anyone and Roux has done nothing other than
try to help me. Please, give me the chance to
prove I'm harmless.

Smooth Sailing,
Gauge the Apprentice

The Healer drops the note to her lap. It's wrong, what's happening to the boy. There isn't any evidence that he's dangerous. If he really calls the Wolf, how has everyone around him survived all these winters? She thinks back to the boy's gentle eyes, his fierce determination.

Something tells her that there is more to the story— maybe even more than the boy knows. She can't help but think of Avril, of his endless devotion to Mistress Vulpine's memory, his obsession with setting the boy out to sea. Something about it doesn't feel quite right.

For far too long, she's stood by, looked the other way as he used his position to enrich himself, to increase his power. Avril has never been flexible once he charts his course, but this is one battle worth fighting.

She tugs on a housecoat, snatches the candle, and hurries across the square.

She pounds on the door until Lord Mayor Vulpine's Keeper pulls it open, her eyes heavy with sleep.

"Whatever are you doing here at this hour?" the Keeper says. "Come in, come in."

"I'd like to see the children at once," the Healer says.

"I'm afraid that's quite impossible. Lord Mayor Vulpine ordered—"

"He'll get over it," the Healer calls back, already hurrying upstairs.

Outside the prisoners' room, the Guards hesitate only briefly before allowing the Healer access. Hearing the commotion, Lord Mayor Vulpine stumbles from his sleeping room. He attempts to smooth his hair, which sticks up in disarray. "What in the Seven Seas is going on?"

He sees the Healer through the open door. "Nicoline! What are *you* doing here?"

She puts a hand on her hip. "Is that any way to greet your big sister?"

"Most sisters wouldn't come barging into their

brothers' houses in the middle of the night, interfering with official business," he mutters.

"I think we established long ago that I'm not like most sisters," the Healer retorts. She turns to a stunned Gauge and Roux.

"How are you two holding up? I trust my brother has kept you comfortable?"

Gauge and Roux stare at her, confused.

The Healer waves Gauge's note in the air. "Can either of you tell me how this came to be on my bedside table?"

The boy's gaze slides to where I stand next to the Healer. I nod encouragingly.

"Um, the Wolf delivered it," Gauge says.

"The Wolf?" Lord Mayor Vulpine whirls, searching the room. "Where is it? Is it here?"

"She's there, beside the Healer," the boy says.

Lord Mayor Vulpine's face drains of blood. He backs away from his sister.

"I knew it," he says to Gauge. "I knew you could call the Wolf."

"Oh, put a cork in it," his sister says. "He's a Voyant. Of course he calls the Wolf."

"Actually, I can't call—"

"He murdered my wife!" Lord Mayor Vulpine says, his voice shaking.

"I did not!" Gauge says.

"You called the Wolf to your shop the day she set sail."

"I did no such thing," Gauge sputters. "I was as surprised to see the Wolf as you were to hear about it."

"So you deny that you caused my wife's death?"

"I absolutely deny it. The Wolf didn't cause your wife's death either—she doesn't cause anyone's death. She helps them get to the Woods Beyond."

"A bunch of nonsense if I've ever heard any. Prove it."

"What proof do you have of *your* accusations?" the Healer asks Lord Mayor Vulpine.

He stutters, "I—I'm the Lord Mayor of this village, granted authority by Grand Lord Lasage himself."

"Yes, yes, yes," the Healer says. "We've heard it all before. What would Mother say, were she here now? She raised us to follow the letter and, more importantly, the *spirit* of the law."

Lord Mayor Vulpine snarls. "The boy is a Voyant. He admitted it himself. We always set them out to sea.

Always." (It's easier for him to believe he set actual Voyants out to sea than to face the atrocities he's committed.)

"Because we've always done things a certain way doesn't mean we can't change," the Healer says coolly.

"How do we know the boy isn't dangerous?" Lord Mayor Vulpine asks. "How do we know he's telling the truth?"

Gauge chews on his lip as all eyes in the room fall on him.

"Make him an offer he can't refuse," I say.

The boy shakes his head, not understanding.

"Tell him you can give him news of his wife."

"His *wife*?" Gauge asks.

"What do you know of my wife?" Lord Mayor Vulpine asks.

"Tell him she had an easy passing," I say.

"Your wife had an easy passing," Gauge says.

"How do you know?" Lord Mayor Vulpine's voice cracks.

"Tell him she was one of the stronger souls I ever carried. That Mother Wolf sent her to the Woods Beyond almost immediately."

The boy repeats my words.

"Lies," Lord Mayor Vulpine shouts. "All lies!" His cheeks glisten.

"Tell him her passing isn't his fault."

"He doesn't think it's his fault," Gauge says. "He thinks it's *my* fault."

"Tell him!"

"The Wolf says—" The boy takes a deep breath. "She says Mistress Vulpine's passing wasn't your fault."

For a moment, the room feels as though it's been emptied of air.

Lord Mayor Vulpine sinks to his knees. "It was an accident," he says. "A horrible accident. I didn't mean for her to trip on my cane."

"Your cane?" the Healer gasps.

Lord Mayor Vulpine's shoulders shake with silent sobs.

"She was always after me to put it up. If only I'd listened . . ." He's too overcome to continue.

The Healer crosses the room and rests a hand on his shoulder. "It was her time." She glances at Gauge and continues. "There is nothing that you—or anyone else—could have done to stop it."

Lord Mayor Vulpine's face has turned red and puffy.

The Healer continues quietly. "Grief often cloaks itself in anger. But you can't continue blaming this boy for your loss."

Lord Mayor Vulpine struggles to catch his breath. "What would you have me do—tell the people I was wrong?"

"If necessary," the Healer says.

"I can't do that."

"Then perhaps it's time the people know about your little arrangement with Ruben the Vessel-maker. How you use your position—and their taxes—to line your own pockets. Not to mention those of your friends." This time, the Healer's voice has an edge to it.

"No! Please!" Lord Mayor Vulpine crawls toward her, clings to her ankles.

"Then let these children go."

"No. I can't."

The Healer shakes him off. The flame on her candle flickers, threatening to plunge them into darkness before steadying. "Then I shall tell the villagers the truth."

Lord Mayor Vulpine attempts to draw himself up. "They'll never believe you."

"They may *fear* you, but they *respect* me," she says.

"You wouldn't dare!"

"Try me."

Lord Mayor Vulpine sees that he's beat. He buries his face in his hands, sobbing.

The Healer softens. "You might find it easier to let go of those who have set sail if you learn to take comfort in the living."

Lord Mayor Vulpine wails.

The Healer calls for the Guards. They enter, their torches blazing, swords drawn. "That's hardly necessary," she says.

Sheepishly, they sheathe their swords.

She motions toward Gauge and Roux. "Please see to it these two arrive safely back at the smithy."

She addresses the children. "Tomorrow my brother will issue a statement clearing you of all wrongdoing."

Roux and Gauge squeeze hands, hardly able to believe their change in fortune.

"What about the Wolf?" Gauge asks.

"What about it?"

"The villagers should know that she's not dangerous. She's . . . she's my friend." (I don't need to tell you
how these words make me feel.)

"I don't doubt it," the Healer says. "But change
comes slowly. And I'm not sure the people of Bouge
are ready to welcome an invisible Great White Wolf
into their midst."

I pad over to the boy and nuzzle his hand with my
nose. "I don't mind."

"Someday," he promises, resting his hand on my
head, "we'll tell them the truth. Make them accept
you."

Someday. Not long ago, spending one more day on
the job would have filled me with dread. My daughter
is still waiting in the Woods Beyond. And I still long
to see her with every bit of my heart. But affection
shines from the boy's eyes. Suddenly, someday doesn't
sound all that bad.

The smell of licorice and tobacco interrupts my
thoughts.

Gauge notices me sniffing. "You have to go, don't
you?"

"Duty calls."

He drops his hand. "When will I see you again?"

"You don't have to worry about that." I give my coat a good shake. "I'll be around."

The last thing I see before I disappear is a smile spreading across his face.

When Gauge and Roux leave the Lord Mayor's home, they find a young woman hunched on his front stairs nursing a baby. She looks up at them with eyes full of pain.

"Is it true?" she whispers in a wobbly voice.

The boy isn't sure how to answer.

"My husband, he set sail last week. Is it true that Lord Mayor Vulpine made a deal with the Wolf?" Tears glint on her cheeks.

She looks up at the sky. The clouds have passed and the lanterns shine brightly overhead. "If he didn't reach the Sea, then what happened to him?"

Gauge winces as the woman's raw pain cuts through him. It's like his own anguish when he realized the Release was a sham. Or the grief on Roux's face when he told her the Wolf stole her father. Losing a loved one is hard enough when you believe they sailed on to somewhere safe, somewhere free of life's pain and struggles. The name's not important—whether you call it the Woods Beyond or the Sea-in-the-Sky, what matters is the comfort that believing brings.

Gauge descends the stairs and sinks down next to the woman. "I was wrong," he says. "There is no deal."

He stops, wondering what to say next, how much to tell the woman. He guesses she's not ready for a discussion about the Woods Beyond. "Your husband, he's waiting for you."

The boy points at the lights twinkling above. "I don't know if any of these lanterns are his, but I do know he's counting the moments until you join him."

The woman strokes her infant's cheek. The baby takes a break from feeding to gurgle and coo. "Not too soon, I hope," the woman says.

The air smells of spring rain, of new beginnings. "None of us know when our time will come," the boy says. "But I suspect you have nothing to worry about."

"Thank you," the woman says, burying her face in the small puff of hair on top of her baby's head.

Gauge runs his hand through his own hair. He doesn't know if everyone in Gatineau will continue on with their traditions, doesn't know if *he'll* want to follow the traditions. He knows now that it's not necessary, but someday, he might want to have his head shaved. The idea no longer bothers him as it once did. He can't put into words the changes that have taken place inside him, and indeed, it will take him several winters to heal, to look back on these days with clarity.

For the moment, he feels a softening in his chest, a small flame melting a bit of the ice that formed around his heart after his grandpapá's death. The boy is ready to experience life again—to embrace its joys and its sorrows. To cycle through its continual beginnings and endings, its hellos and goodbyes.

Again, he takes in the dots twinkling overhead. This time, he understands: without the dark, the lanterns wouldn't shine.

One of the Guards behind him shuffles, encouraging Gauge to move on. (The Guard's shift ends soon and he's eager to complete this task so he can go home to his new wife.)

The boy rises and offers Roux his elbow. "Shall we?"

She accepts his arm, and together, they disappear down the street.

Chapter Sixteen

The next day, Gauge stands in front of his grandpapá's shop with Roux and Yanis, who had greeted them when they returned to the smithy late the night before. They had caught him up on recent events, and though he was initially wary of Gauge, the sturdy, soft-spoken boy quickly warmed up, stating that any friend of Roux's was a friend of his. Yanis insisted on accompanying Gauge and Roux to the carpentry shop in case they ran into any problems.

Luckily, someone had cleaned up the broken glass and nailed wood across the open window. Gauge takes a deep breath.

"Are you sure you're up for this?" Roux reaches for her hair, but then she stops herself and places a supportive hand on the boy's arm.

"No sense putting it off." He pushes open the door and steps inside. His grandpapá's voice calls from the workshop, but when Gauge blinks, there is only an empty counter, darkness, and silence.

In the back, each of the old man's tools are neatly stacked, his unfinished work waiting. Gauge runs his fingers over the smooth pine leg of the dining table that was his grandpapá's final project. It's for the Butcher.

The boy considers keeping the table for himself. But no. His grandpapá would want the job finished, the table delivered as promised. The boy moves to his grandpapá's tools. He grips the handle of his grandpapá's best hacksaw, marvels at how it fits perfectly in his hand.

Yanis moves deeper into the room, bends, and pulls something from under a worktable. "What's this?"

Gauge's breath catches. He pushes the wooden boat across the table, thinking of the hours he played with it in front of the fire with his grandpapá looking on. Those days—when his biggest worry was carving a fisherman to work the ship—feel like a hundred winters ago. The game that once felt so important now seems childish. But he'll keep the boat all the same. Someday, when he has wee ones of his own, he'll share it with them and tell them about the best grandpapá anyone could ever have.

The boy sets down the boat and moves toward the living room.

He pushes open the door. The room is smaller than he remembers, quieter. He breathes in the lingering smell of wood shavings, of potatoes, of his grandpapá.

He crosses the room and spots his folding knife on the floor. He scoops it up, relishing the comfortable fit in his palm. Bending, he pulls the mostly finished fisherman from under the bed. Flicking open the blade, he rests his thumb on the figurine's chest and pulls his knife toward him, shaving off a small flake of basswood and revealing a curl in the carving's hair.

A rush of satisfaction floods Gauge as his hand continues guiding the blade. The boy feels his grandpapá beside him, sees the old man nod his approval. Each curl slowly takes shape. His grandpapá was right: there's no resisting the call of the wood.

Roux pushes open a curtain, bathing the room

in golden sunlight. Outside the window, green buds blooming on the rosebush hint of the summer to come. Roux offers Gauge a small smile and he smiles back, wishing his grandpapá had gotten to know her.

While Yanis brushes the cobwebs from the hearth and starts a fire, I nudge open the door, pad inside, and nuzzle Gauge's elbow. He startles and then snaps the knife shut. Grinning, he scratches behind my ears.

"Couldn't stay away?"

I snort, but there's some truth to his words. As unbelievable as it sounds, I'm bound to death but determined to help Gauge enjoy the rest of his life. As we catch up, a knock sounds on the back door.

The boy opens it cautiously.

"Might I come in?" Nicoline the Healer asks.

"Of course!" Gauge says, pulling the door open. As she enters, he frets. "I'm afraid I only have tea to offer."

"I figured as much." The Healer pulls a pack off her shoulder and unloads a loaf of crusty bread, butter, and a jar of lavender-laced honey.

The boy's mouth waters.

"And here's something to throw on the fire." She unwraps a filet of fresh cod.

The question Gauge wanted to ask his grandpapá comes back to him. As he moves closer to the fire, he can't help but think that maybe cod was the old man's favorite.

I pad after him. "It was your mother's favorite, actually."

Gauge's hands tremble as he drops the cod in the pan, where it sizzles in protest.

"It wasn't true, by the way," I say.

"What wasn't true?"

"What I said about her taking my job. I couldn't have convinced her to leave you if I'd had all the time in the world."

Gauge nods as he wipes his hands. He suspected as much, but he needed to hear it.

The Healer pulls another package from her bag. "I also brought some smoked eel."

Gauge pauses. Our gazes meet. I see that he already knows. He realizes he knew all along. The boy remembers his grandpapá smearing smoked eel across a piece of rye bread, remembers the old man lifting it to his mouth and declaring that if he were ever given one last meal, that would be it. The boy remembers answering, "I don't care what my last meal would be, as long as it was with you."

The old man's eyes shined with happiness. With love.

Gauge's vision blurs. He finally understands that his grandpapá was never embarrassed by him. Although the old man was wrong about me, every decision he made was because he loved the boy with all his heart and would have done anything to protect him.

The boy's eyes shimmer as he uses a poker to tend the fire.

The bell rings at the front of the shop, signaling another visitor.

"Who could that be?" Gauge asks.

"There are a million fish in the sea," the Healer says. "Could be any one of them."

The boy enters the shop and hurries to the front counter, followed by Roux, the Healer, and Yanis. A man in sage pantaloons and a bright tunic measures the front window, a small child at his feet.

"Can I help you?" Gauge asks.

The man turns around.

"Snatty!" The boy rushes forward to shake the

Guard's hand. "I'm glad to see you again," he says. "But what are you doing here?"

"Bouge-by-the-Sea has always prided itself on being fair and just. The way we treated you—well, it was wrong and I'm sorry about that."

"I can hardly—"

The man waves for Gauge's silence. "The least we can do is help put your shop back in order."

The boy is speechless.

Snatty gestures to the curly-haired girl on the floor. She sits with her thumb in her mouth. "I hope you don't mind that I brought along a helper."

He digs in his pocket. "Oh, and a collection was taken up to help you pay the Vessel-maker's bill and get back on your feet."

He passes Gauge a bag heavy with shells.

The kindness is too much for the boy, who stands blinking.

"Come on," Roux says. "Let's have a bite to eat before we get to work."

Her words break Gauge's spell. He holds up the bag to Roux. "There's enough here for both of us."

"Actually, there's one more thing," the Healer says, clearing her throat.

"What's that?" Gauge asks.

"I'm in need of an Apprentice." She addresses Roux. "Are you interested?"

"Interested?" Roux flings her arms around the Healer's shoulders. "There's nothing I'd like better!"

At first the Healer stiffens, but then she softens and wraps her arms around Roux. After a moment, she breaks away. "Enough of that," she says. "Somebody better tend the fish or we'll be having charcoal."

Gauge trails the group back into his grandpapá's living room—his living room now. A shadow rests on his shoulders, memories of his grandpapá, longing for what might have been had the old man lived. But with each moment that passes, the boy's burden grows lighter. He'll never stop missing his grandpapá, but he'll live a long, happy life, surrounded by people who aren't the family he was born into but who love him all the same. And he'll love them right back.

I settle down in front of the fire, content for the first time in seven hundred winters. Of course I'm still eager to rejoin my daughter. And I feel terrible that I tried to trick the boy. This job would be fine for someone old, someone without an entire life yet to live. Somehow, I ache less than before our adventure began. It turns out that as my heart heals, so does my body.

The next time I smell licorice-scented tobacco in the air, I'll be ready. And who knows, maybe someday another Voyant will come my way. If that ever happens, I'll offer them my job—after telling them all about it.

(I'd consider offering you the position, but you are far too young. And apparently only citizens of Gatineau are eligible. I can't figure out how you could possibly be a Voyant in the first place. Perhaps you have a relative from here. A long-lost cousin? An aunt? There must be some connection.)

Eighty-Three Winters Later . . .

The Carpenter rocks gently in his favorite hickory chair. Embers glow red-hot in the fireplace, remnants of a once roaring fire. The air smells of licorice, of tobacco. I settle down beside the old man. Ninety-five winters have turned his once-curly hair sparse and silver, his skin thin and wrinkled.

"You sure about this?" I ask.

The Carpenter has lived a good life. He recently lost his wife of seventy-two winters, but if there's one thing Roux taught him, it's never to pass up an adventure. Together, they traveled far outside of Gatineau, saw more than they ever would have believed possible. He wishes he could share this next leg of his journey with her, too, but he knows that when he finally arrives in the Woods Beyond, she'll be waiting to hear all about it.

There's no hurry. After all, what's a few hundred winters when all of eternity stretches in front of them? He scratches under my chin. "I'm sure," he says. "You've earned your retirement."

It's true. After nearly eight hundred winters, I've done my part. It's time for me to move on, to finally make my journey to the Woods Beyond. Warmth fills my chest as I imagine Émilie jumping into my arms and burying her face in my neck.

"What are you waiting for?" the old man asks.

I take one last look around his living room. I'll miss the warmth of the fire and the friendship I shared with him, but I'm ready.

"Give me your hand," I say.

He stretches out a frail hand dotted with age. I run my tongue over his palm. It tastes of sunshine, wood, the sea—a life well-lived. The old man's eyes fall shut. A comfortable heaviness spreads through my limbs. I settle on the floor as the light fades around me.

My daughter's voice echoes through the distance, through the winters. "Mama," she calls. "Mama, where are you?"

"I'm coming," I whisper. "I'll be there soon."

The old man's body tingles with a curious sensation. It's not quite pain, but it's not entirely comfortable, either. He feels himself stretching, twisting, bending, growing. His skin tingles as thick white fur pushes its way out. His ears sharpen, then twitch. He's overwhelmed with the sounds that surround him, once mute but now shockingly vibrant—a spider creeping across the window, the Potter's voice murmuring next door, the roar of the sea.

But it's the intense smell—black licorice and tobacco—that makes him open his eyes. He's standing on four paws, a fluffy tail swishing behind him.

A crone lies on the floor, her long silver hair shimmering in the fading light. Her eyes are closed, her chest still. Her graceful hands are folded peacefully over her stomach.

"Alouette," the Wolf murmurs. He bows his head

respectfully. He didn't want to take this job when it was first offered—not when he had a whole life ahead of him. But now it's a gift, an opportunity. To see more of the world, to serve his beloved community. They took him in, supported his craft, over the many winters offered friendship, love, and laughter.

After the Steward pushed out Lord Mayor Vulpine, life improved for everyone. Businesses flourished, the village grew and changed. Some of its residents insist on holding on to the old ways—performing Releases, watching for their loved ones to light lanterns in the Sea-in-the-Sky. But many of them accept Gauge's story, feel the truth in his words. The two beliefs now coexist, though more villagers open their hearts and minds with each passing day.

The Wolf wants to linger, to spend another moment or two in this space between his old life and the new one that awaits him. But his instincts drive him forward, guide him to the crone's feet. He runs his tongue across her wrinkled sole and then tugs gently. A warm ball of golden light slides out, squirming like a pup eager for its first meal. The

Wolf secures the soul between his teeth and, with a last glance at the room he's always called home, follows the comforting scent of milk toward the den, eager to help Alouette join her daughter in the Woods Beyond.

Acknowledgments

I want to first offer my deepest thanks to everyone who played a role in helping me share this story with readers. I'll be forever indebted to my editor, Martha Mihalick, for falling in love with my sweet boy and snarky wolf and providing them a literary home; to my agent, Sara Crowe, for championing me and my work; and to my literary godmother, Erin Entrada Kelly, who waved her magic wand and changed my life. I'd also like to thank the rest of the Greenwillow and HarperCollins teams, including Virginia Duncan, Lois Adams, Paul Zakris, Arianna Robinson, Kim Stella, Vanessa Nuttry, Emma Meyer, and Jacquelynn Burke, as well as my freelance copy editor, Sarah Thomson.

In addition, I'd like to acknowledge the artistry of Anna and Elena Balbusso, creators of my extraordinary cover.

It truly takes a village to write a book and, after fourteen years of striving for publication, my village might be larger than most. Thank you to the 21ders and the Class of 2k21, who have been instrumental in helping me navigate this year's many ups and downs. I also owe a special note of thanks to the following: my dear friend Rebecca Petruck for her thoughtful insights—without them, I might never have found the Wolf's voice (or the heart of the story); Julie Artz, who, besides being a terrific friend, critique partner, and mind-melding co-mentor, helped me jump into the world of fantasy even though I wasn't sure it was where I belonged; Eileen Schnabel, who has walked by my side through the entire journey, encouraging me to stay centered and believing in my future success even when it felt out of reach; and Saba Sulaiman, who was the first to take a chance on me and helped turn me into the writer I am today.

Susan Berk Koch, Juliana Brandt, Gabrielle Byrne, Tara Creel, Cory Leonardo, Yael Mermelstein, Kate

Foster, Reese Eschmann, Gita Trelease, Niki Lenz, Tiffany Liu, Kurt Hartwig, Seda Oz, Krista Fiolleau, Melynda Pomeroy, Kelly Gonsalves, Bette Castanier, Sue Langdon, Sandra Owen, Dr. Robert Miller, Dr. Srikumar Rao, Lissa McLaughlin, Angela Rydell, Christine DeSmet, members of The Winged Pen, the Pitch Wars community, and everyone else who provided thoughtful feedback on this or my other projects over the years: thank you. (Jaiden Vitalis—I definitely owe you a pony!)

I would be remiss if I didn't also take this opportunity to thank the many people who offered critical support during difficult periods in my life. It would be impossible to name you all individually, but each and every one of you have my everlasting gratitude. In particular, I'd like to thank the Currier, Pickerd, Havener, Wagner, and Eggert families. Deb Elkin, thank you for helping me transform my monsters into something more manageable. Duenows and Mechunkels, thank you for the adventures, friendship, laughter, and love. To my mother, Carolyn Stout, as well as Jamie, Sarah, Casey, Ben, and Grandma Florine: despite the miles that separate us, I carry you all in my heart.

Adam, Jaiden, and Sienna, thank you for encouraging me to follow my dreams, for telling me those early drafts "didn't suck" (even though they did), and for teaching me to love wholeheartedly and without reserve—you are the bright, shining lanterns that light my life. (Boop!)